THE WET WALKERS

THE WET WALKERS
VOLUME 2

MARY SMITH

The Wet Walkers

Copyright © 2020 by Mary Smith. All rights reserved.

No part of this publication may be reproduced, stored in a retrieval system or transmitted in any way by any means, electronic, mechanical, photocopy, recording or otherwise without the prior permission of the author except as provided by USA copyright law.

The opinions expressed by the author are not necessarily those of URLink Print and Media.

1603 Capitol Ave., Suite 310 Cheyenne, Wyoming USA 82001
1-888-980-6523 | admin@urlinkpublishing.com

URLink Print and Media is committed to excellence in the publishing industry.

Book design copyright © 2020 by URLink Print and Media. All rights reserved.

Published in the United States of America

ISBN 978-1-64753-483-7 (Paperback)
ISBN 978-1-64753-485-1 (Hardback)
ISBN 978-1-64753-486-8 (Digital)

21.10.20

This series of beloved books
are dedicated with
gratitude

for the love and life
of

Ralph Messick Smith II

~ my favorite "wet walker"

CHAPTER 1

I don't know for sure how long those "wimmin" sat talkin' and rockin' in front of that cozy little fire, but I know my heart was peaceful watchin' 'em as I drifted off. My three Mams. My three Mams. And my little Mam is safe and maybe when I had my angel shiver, she was gettin' her wings. I wondered why on earth I'd been so scared about all the people comin'. I just wasn't usin' my melon, cuz I have so many folks lovin' me and lookin' out for me I shouldn't have worried at all. I'm sure glad God-Willin' has *patience* with little ones like me and has lots of folk around me that are reminders. Seems like if they're all busy, why he'll just remind me himself. I sure remembered to say my prayers tonight and I included my Martha. I wish I could hold my eyes open a little longer but tomorrow will be a busy day and I'll be meetin' lots of new folks, so I need to be ready.

—∞—

The three women sat by the fire and drank cups of hot tea that Raff had brought in. They chatted quietly and seemed to have established a comfortable bond. Just loving Lil would have been bond enough, but their friendship seemed deep enough to touch all of them in their corners, with joy and sadness. Raff and Martha seemed especially close. They were only a year apart in age and had grown up in similar times, in like situations. Oatie found herself floating in and out of a dream-like state. The reality of her future was near. She knew she should be sewing on her wedding dress, simple though it was, but she felt if the other women were anything like Martha was telling them to expect, she'd have many hands at work helping her to get ready. She could tell that Raff and Martha were kindred spirits, they talked and laughed and shared stories as though they'd grown up together. She loved watching the two of them. Martha was sharing her life with Raff, telling her about William, who sounded much like Raff's Jim and about the joy of Billy Joe and the sadness of not having others. It almost seemed like a slight grimace of pain would appear on Martha's face from time to time, but Oatie disregarded it, since she didn't know Martha well enough to be familiar with her facial expressions. She decided it was the shadows from the little fire dancing around and playing games on all their faces. They all hated to call it a night, but the three seemed to sense the other's timing and prepared for their night in easy fashion. They embraced each other as old friends might and snuggled into their respective beds.

Oatie went to the night secure in knowing the blessing of this gathering. Raff closed her eyes with the contented knowledge of meeting a new friend – unexpected, but soon to be cherished as another sister. She wondered silently if she had imagined those few looks on Martha's countenance. The lovely firelight was dancing on all their faces and playing its own tricks. Surely, it was only her imagination. She closed her eyes as she thanked God for all that was coming, but especially for her new friend, Martha Bailey.

Martha Bailey was overcome with the goodness of God. Her heart, mind and soul were at once peaceful. He in his goodness had allowed her to find the person she needed. She could now proceed with her plans. She felt a surge of energy and … excitement going through her body. She would sleep well tonight.

I sat straight up in bed. There was a new fire hopping around in the fireplace as though to say, wake up, sleepyhead, this is your biggest day. I knew somethin' had awakened me and then I heard sounds – so loud, people calling and whistlin' and laughing. I could hear horses and wagons. I'd never heard so much noise in my lifetime. I was alone, but the door was held open a crack with a carefully placed brick. It wasn't black night, it was early first light. I hopped out of bed and ran to the door to see if I could see where the voices were comin' from. Down by the cook fire were groups of people talkin' to each other, slappin' each other on the back and laughin' and in the middle of 'em was Oatie and Raff and Martha. They were cookin' and stirrin', pourin' coffee and fryin' bacon. Uncle Fury was talkin' and pointin' towards all the rocks, and it was so excitin' I could hardly get my breath.

I wanted to be in it, a part of it. I needed to find my clothes and get down there. Everyone was shiverin' a little from the early mornin' chill, but they were rubbin' their hands together over the giant fire and stampin' their boots and talkin' and laughin' and teasin' each other. It looked so happy I couldn't stand it. I ran back to our bed and sure enough there was a brand new pair of overalls and a bright green flannel shirt I'd never seen. There was some new knit green socks and a warm undershirt and long underpants. I got my business taken care of, the bed all straight and the pillows fluffed. I ran to the water pitcher and took my little cloth and washed my face. It wouldn't do at all to go meet all these new happy people with the face of a sleepyhead. I left my hands a little wet and frizzled them through my curls so they'd know to bounce into place, and I was ready to go.

All of a sudden I got a shy lump in my throat. I went runnin' over to the linen press and sat on the floor and pulled out the box where Miss Myrtle was havin' her "vacation." I missed her and I knew she missed me, but it was better that my child was safe. I could tell her about everythin' that happened later. I could tell she was happy to see me and was proud that I was goin' to meet these new people. Just holdin' her gave me the courage I needed and the shy lump was completely gone. I was pushin' her back into place when I heard the brick move and Oatie come creepin' in. Her face was wreathed with smiles and her eyes was shinin'. She spotted me and gave me a big hug and asked how Miss Myrtle was. I told her about my shy lump and how Miss Myrtle made it go away and I couldn't wait to get out by the fire.

Oatie laughed, hugged me again and said, "Lil, I'm so-o-o proud of you. You've put the room in order and dressed yourself and even tended to your face. Do you like your new things? That green shirt is a showstopper. Green is certainly your color."

I said, "Oatie, when you come out with new sayin's, I have to ponder 'em. I know if you're sayin' them, they're good things but I have to think on 'em till they make sense to me. A showstopper … what in the world? Can I have other colors than green, or do I just get one?"

She was gigglin' and she made me giggle too.

She said, "Lil, that melon of yours sure never stops. The 'showstopper' means something appears to be so fine that everyone has to stop to admire it, and yes, all God's colors belong to each of us. You just happen to look exceptionally beautiful to me right now, and green happens to look so pretty with your red curls bouncin' in the firelight. Oh Lil, let's go meet all these new grand people. This is so much fun. They're all eating breakfast and putting up tents and unloading wagons. Oh my, it is SO exciting. They expect Billy Joe, his dad and the other wagons in an hour or so. There are people everywhere, Lil. It's just the most exciting thing I've ever been a part of. The people are dear and they certainly seem to be impressed with your Uncle Fury. Lands, you'd think he'd known them all forever. I'm going to grab one of our warmer shawls for Martha. Hers is too light for this early mornin' air. You best pull on your little sweater for a while. Clay can't wait to show his "little sister and first friend" off to everyone. I would have let you sleep a little longer, but he's about badgered me to pieces. Let's go get you something warm in your tummy. Martha has saved a place for you on the bench beside her."

We walked out the front door. Oatie pushed the brick aside and pulled the door to and we started down the stairs. Clay came runnin' up and grabbed my hands, and we jigged around in a circle. He was laughin' and said, "Isn't this just the best, Lil? Come meet Roy Jack. He's my age and he's grand. His sister Rebecca is fun, too. She's about twelve or so and ..." he whispered in my ear, "she's kind of bossy!"

"Clay, what's that mean exactly?" I said.

Clay looked around and then giggled and said, "She likes to tell everyone what to do. Roy Jack just waves his hand at her, grins and says to pay her no mind. We're sittin' across from Martha – she's saved you a seat beside her. Come on, I'll help you carry your breakfast."

Oatie had a bowl of grits ready for me and a big piece of warm bread and butter and a couple of big pieces of bacon. She handed Clay my cup of milk and the bowl of grits. I carried my bread and bacon. Martha took it out of my hands, laid it on the table in front of me and helped me climb up on the bench beside her. She smelled so good that I leaned over and nuzzled her. She put her arm around me and tucked her shawl around my shoulders. She kissed my curls and said, "Good morning, Mary Sunshine."

I thought for a minute she'd forgotten my name, but she was already chuckling and sayin', "My Mother greeted me every morning of my life with those very words. When I was little, I'd get all worried for fear she'd forgotten my name. Then I went through a period where I thought it was my name instead of Martha. When I finally got it all straight, I decided it was the perfect way to say good mornin' to someone you love."

Clay was spoonin' in his grits but he stopped and looked at her, he grinned and said, "What did you say to Billy Joe?"

We all laughed, and Martha said, "I'm gonna let you all ask Billy Joe." She had a twinkle in her eye and I was lovin' this breakfast time.

I finished my breakfast and was about to hop down and run after Clay and meet that bossy girl and maybe even get to watch her "boss," when I felt Martha pat me. She smiled and said, "I was hoping you could spend some time with me and we could get acquainted."

I looked at those kids as Clay ran up to 'em and they all started talkin' with each other. I wanted to go so-o-o bad, almost more than anythin', but as I looked back at Martha's sweet smile, all of a sudden

I remembered my "doin' better" and how bad I'd made my sweet animals feel when I ignored them by doin' what I wanted to do. She made me think of my sweet Dancer and little innocent Willy and Nelly. I gave a mighty big sigh, but I threw my arms around Martha, gave her sweet smellin' cheek a kiss, and showed her my dimple.

She told me so many wonderful stories that I didn't know time had passed or that people, people, people were millin' around. Raff brought her a hot cup of tea and me one, too! Mine had sugar and hot milk and I loved it. She patted my head and went back to the cook fire surrounded by wimmin who was, *were* helpin' with the cookin'. I couldn't take my eyes off of Martha. She made me laugh, she showed me tricks that made me clap, she made my heart hurt so that I almost cried, but she always made me end up laughin'. I never ever had such a good time.

We were interrupted by lots of yellin' and laughin' and the sounds of horses and wagons pullin' in near the upper pasture. Shouts, whistles, and horses snortin' had everybody runnin' past us.

Even Oatie and Raff came over to us and said, "Ladies, shall we go participate in the start of our new world?"

Martha looked at me, smilin', and said, "Would you like that, Miss Lil?"

I said, "Oh yes please." I jumped off the bench and waited for Martha to get up and adjust her stole. I took her hand and Oatie's and we started up the path to the trail. Raff grabbed Martha's other arm and they began to chat.

When we got to where the trail comes into our unloadin' area, there were wagons as far as my eyes could see, and drivin' the first one was Billy Joe. He spotted us, waved his hat at us, handed the reins to another gentlemen, hopped down and headed for us. He was grinnin' that grin, and he loped down and picked his Mother up and swung her around. She squealed with delight as he kissed her and grabbed me up and swung me, nuzzled my neck and planted a big kiss on my dimple. He said, "Good morning to all my beautiful Mary Sunshines." I gasped and started laughin'. Martha did too. He said, "Mother, what do you think of my girlfriend?"

She said, "I'm grateful for your extraordinary good taste, of course, I can't seem to get enough of her."

Everyone seemed to be talking at once, and there were so many folks jabberin' and howdyin' that I could hardly make sense of it all, but I knew Martha and Billy Joe both loved me and that made my insides so warm, and my outsides shine with happiness.

A tall man, a handsome tall man, even taller than Billy Joe and Uncle Fury, came up to us, swept his hat off, bowed and said, "Ladies, and Martha my love. It looks to me like we've moved Middleboro into the prettiest part of Kentucky I've seen yet."

Uncle Fury came up to us and shook hands with the big bear of a man. They grasped each other and smiled as good friends do, and Fury said, "William, thanks for helping with this undertaking. It was a surprise to see you in wagon number two and your rascal of a son in the lead wagon!"

The big bear man laughed with his eyes and his mouth and said, "I figured he might as well learn the ropes on your nickel, Fury. Saves me paying for any mistakes he might make."

Everyone sure seemed to think that was funny except me. I sure didn't like anyone pickin' on my Billy Joe or laughin' at him. I tightened my hold around his neck and turned his face so my eyes could look into his. I put my finger on his nose and told him NOT to get upset by their laughin'.

He looked right at the bear and Uncle Fury and said, "You two might want to think twice before pickin' on me. My girlfriend doesn't like it, and I want you to know she's a force to be reckoned with."

Uncle Fury and the bear man walked over real close to us. "William," Uncle Fury said, "let me introduce you to my er, ah, sweet and beautiful daughter Lil, who by the way seems to have captured your son's heart, along with everyone who meets her."

William, or Bear Man, focused his eyes right on my eyes and pulled on his beard. He had a huge bunch of hair that came to his shoulders like Billy Joe's. But, where Billy Joe's was yellow blond, the bear man seemed to have more, plus a big moustache like Uncle

Fury's and a beard. His hair seemed to be whitish, but looked like it remembered being yellow.

He walked slowly towards me, and I tightened my hold on Billy Joe. When he was right across from us, he was still lookin' down on us a little. Mercy, but he was a big bear of a man. He stopped pullin' on his beard, clapped Billy Joe on his shoulder, which should have hurt, and leaned close. His eyes looked into mine and he said, "Miss Lil, sounds like you and me need to become fast friends. You see, you've got your Uncle Fury and Billy Joe, and I've heard they've given you some mighty fine shoulder pony rides around camp. But little darlin', I'm the King of pony rides! You'll be way higher than they can get you, and I'm lots stronger than those two little rascals. So how about givin' me a chance?"

He cocked his head, and his face and eyes burst into the purtiest grin ever. He made me want to jump up and down and laugh and clap my hands – I just loved him. He held his arms out. I kissed Billy Joe on the cheek and threw myself into them. He held me a minute while we studied each other. He finally said, "What would you like to call me, sweetheart?"

I didn't wait a minute. I was already laughin', and I said, "Uncle Bear."

Everyone joined in as he threw his head back and roared with laughter. This was a happy time. He took his big gentle hands and lifted me up on the biggest shoulders I'd ever been on. I was so high up it almost made me dizzy.

Uncle Fury walked over and took Oatie and Raff's hands and drew them over to us. He said, "Ladies, this is my fine friend, William Bailey, father of a rascal named Billy Joe Bailey and the husband of our sainted Martha." Oatie and Raff did some beautiful curtsy things and they made me so proud. I loved my family and I loved this Bailey family too.

I remembered when I first started my livin' again, I heard Oatie and Raff sayin' how they were "feelin' in their bones." I wished over and over I would get big enough to do that, whatever it was. Well I'm guessin' I must be almost grown up, because I'm gettin' "feelin's in my bones."

Oatie, Raff and Martha were walkin' towards the box house and our cook fire arm in arm, gabbin' like they'd all grown up together. I was ridin' on Uncle Bear's shoulder with Uncle Fury and Billy Joe on either side of us. It was wonderful bein' up this high. I could see people swarmin' like bees, carryin' logs to be sliced, hookin' up pull sleds, changin' into groups that were startin' to carry them on to different spots. Some were headin' for the lower pasture and others to the barn to be built. There was a group right at our box house layin' boards out for the storage area. Another great big group was startin' on the foundation for our new box house. Smaller bunches were checkin' papers and layin' out all the Wet Walker cabins. My men folk were talkin' about all the plans and how when everything was completed, then and only then, could they start on the meetin', school, and bizness house. Whew, there were so many words I'd never heard and so much I didn't understand. The men stopped for a minute and it almost seemed like they'd forgotten I was there.

Uncle Fury grabbed Uncle Bear's elbow and said, "Martha ..."

Billy Joe said, "Dad, do you think it was wise to let Mother come up here?"

Uncle Bear put two fingers over his eyebrows and rubbed his forehead. He said, "Let? Let? Are you really saying Let? Good Lord, Billy Joe, where have you been these last twenty years? That would be like tellin' the wind to stop blowin', trees to stop shootin' up, or rivers to stop runnin'. I can't think of anything that would have kept her away ... well, perhaps I could, but I'm not thinking about that, mainly because she won't allow it!"

Billy Joe was starin' at something in the distance ... or nothing. Uncle Fury was looking down at his boot toe, which was diggin' a hole in the dust.

Uncle Bear dragged a big ol' snowy white handkerchief out of his pocket and honked on it. He stuffed it back in his pocket and said to Fury, "Do the ladies know? Oatie and ... Raff?"

Uncle Fury shook his head and said, "No, when Martha told me, she asked me to help keep her secret. I, of course, gave her my promise and would gladly and willingly do anything I could. She asked all about Oatie and seemed so thrilled about our plans to wed. I have to say, when I told her that the whole thing came about because of the strength, good sense and graciousness of her older sister Raff, she became almost excited. She said that her need of a friend like that was a dream she'd held in her heart for a very long time. She told me then that nothing would stop her from coming. My God, William, forgive me if I inspired her to do something that would be detrimental …"

"Don't fret over something you have no control over, Fury, we have total faith in whatever God puts on our plate. Martha, totally, Billy Joe and I …" they looked at each other with love and grinned and he continued "…she'd be surprised and gratified. Somehow I think she knows, she just doesn't discuss it … never pushes it … just lives it."

The women had stopped and were waiting for us to catch up.

Billy Joe reached up and took me off his father's shoulders. He said, "Let me take my gal to the women and, Fury, you show Dad this little beauty spot and the plans, and then we'll go get started. We don't dare miss a minute of daylight."

I had my arms around Billy Joe's neck and I whispered in his ear, "Billy Joe, is my Martha sick?"

Billy Joe stopped and looked in my eyes. He kissed my dimple and said in a low voice, "Yes she is, Lil, but it has to be our secret, all right?"

I nodded my head hard and he continued, "I need to know you'll watch out for her. She loves you and loves to laugh and loves to tell stories and … right now she really needs you."

I patted his face and told him not to worry because I had started my "doin' better" and I would take care of her. I could tell he felt a lot better, and I felt big and important cause I was feelin' in my bones, and I felt needed … and I knew my first secret.

My barn raisin' time didn't turn out to be exactly like I'd been thinkin'. I'd thought I'd get to play all day with the other children, but it seems like no one played much. I guess I woulda been playin' mostly by myself. I just stayed by the fires with the wimmin and worked … mainly, I stayed with Martha. I heard one of the wimmin sayin' Martha seemed to be "feelin' poorly."

I asked Oatie at night to explain all the things I'd heard during the day that didn't make sense to me, and she'd turned her head away and said it simply meant Martha wasn't feeling real well. We mostly whispered, cause even tho Martha went right to sleep after dinner, we mustn't disturb her good rest. She was so wonderful to be with all day that I hardly missed playin'.

Two of the wimmin were workin' on Oatie's wedding dress, and it sure seemed like there was lots of laughin' and cryin'. Martha told me stories, stories, stories. So many I wondered if I would be able to remember them till I was grow'd … grewn … grown … well, till I was big and had a little girl of my own to tell them to. She made me laugh and cry and giggle. I learned about wonders I'd never heard the likes of. She'd been all over our big world. She'd been in cities and seen huge waterfalls and seen mountains so high if you stood at the bottom and looked up at them, you'd surely fall over flat on your back. She and William had gone to U-rup on their honeymoon and met people that spoke different than us. I musta looked mighty puzzled, and she looked at me with her twinklin' eyes and sweet smilin' face, cocked her head and started singin' a little song.

I didn't understand any of the funny words, but all of a sudden my body got stiff and I was frozen with fear … it was that song, that song I knew so well from so long ago, that song … my little Mam had sung to me. Martha was starin' at me and stopped singin'. I could hardly see her through my tears, but I kept my eyes on her as best I could and I hummed the rest of the song, then I said to her, "It's a lullaby, a lullaby of love, from a Mam to her babe."

Martha called to Oatie, who stopped workin' on her weddin' dress and came runnin' over to see if Martha was all right, and then I guess she saw me, and I musta looked funny cause she picked me right up in her arms and started kissin' and shushin' me, and rockin' and pattin' me.

The first thing she always said to me when somethin' weren't, *wasn't* right was how much she loved me, how everything would be all right, and then she'd ask me what was wrong. It gave me thinkin' and gulpin' time so's I could answer her. I managed to mumble, "Th-th-the lull-a-bye, my little Mam's lullaby, Mar-tha just sang it to me in those same funny words. She knows my little Mam's lullaby."

Oatie's eyes darted to Martha's. She smiled sweetly and said, "Martha, we should have told you … our Lil has had quite an unusual beginning to her life. It was frightening, scary at times, but really … quite lovely. Our Lil is quite a special little girl."

She hugged me close again and said softly, "Darlin' child, do you remember that your little Mam, Laura Lee, is found, that she is no longer lost, that she is safely with God-Willin'? That she is with you every minute and is always watchin' over you?"

She started singin' my little song and Martha joined in. They had the purtiest … *prettiest* voices ever and I started hummin' along with them. We was all cryin' real easy like when we finished, but it was the best ever. I thought my heart would bust … *burst*, I was so happy.

They both loved on me and Oatie said, "Martha, what do you think of teachin' our Lil the French words to her lullaby? Then she could sing it whenever she liked, it would shoo away any gloom that tried to crawl in her heart. It would always make her happy when she was feelin' sad."

With tears slowly dryin' on my cheeks, I had to admit it didn't seem to be a happy little lullaby. Then I used my melon and thought – I'm so happy inside I could burst. Then I got to thinking 'bout how my little Mam was sendin' me our song and all of a sudden I figured it wasn't a sad song at all. It was my happy song. She'd sent it through Martha and Oatie to let me know I was loved and that I should be happy. And I was goin' to learn the words! I couldn't help smilin'.

Martha said, "Lil, we are turning this time into quite a happy classroom. We'll have history and geography – that's about all the places far and wide that you'll see someday, and now we'll have a little music class, too. I can't wait. I shall teach you little French songs. Some day, perhaps ... Lil, do you know what a piano is?

I puffed my chest out and said, "I do, I do. Oatie and Raff told me about it, they even drew me a picture of one. My little Mam played one. Martha, did you know I'm learnin' to play the violin? I can play three songs. My Uncle Fury is teachin' me. It's my favorite thing in the world. My little Mam played the violin, too, and she rode her horse. I have my very own horse and her name is Dancer."

I paused to get my breath and Martha said, "Lil, I have a piano and I'm hopin' you and your family will come to Middleboro and stay with us for a week or two and I'll teach you to play the piano. Would you like that?"

I had to get down and jump around and clap my hands. Wasn't this just the best? I was goin' to learn my Mam's lullaby words and songs in that funny talk she liked and hist'ry and jography, and now I was goin' to play the piano.

I said, in all the excitement that I was feelin', "Oh yes, please, Martha, oh thank you, oh yes, please."

She was laughin' and those twinkly eyes was really twinklin', she reached out and grabbed me and hugged me great big and said, "Lil, you're just the medicine I've been needin'."

We were two happy fine friends. I loved my Martha and she loved me right back.

I declare, this is the best barn raisin' I've ever been to!

I live in a big city – my world is so big it scares me! I told Martha I was scared because our lives aren't ever goin' to be the same. I tell Martha everythin'. Next to Clay she's my best friend. She says wimmin just understand wimmin, cause they are wimmin. Martha isn't just a Mam, she's a girl too. I was tryin' to explain this to Clay as he was layin' on his back on the small grassy spot in our garden. (It was our favorite spot, our secret spot where we could talk about things that was goin' on.) I hadn't hardly seen him since our world started changin', but after our noon sandwiches, I saw Oatie and Fury talkin', and she was waggin' her finger up close to his nose.

I heard her say, "He's just a little boy, Fury, and he's overdoing it. He's just ten years old – he's a little boy – he needs his rest, he's exhausted. I am going to get him, and he's coming up here, and he and Lil are going to relax and be with Martha for a couple of hours every day!"

Fury said, "Maybe you're lettin' Martha overdo, did you think of that? Maybe she's worn out."

Oatie brought her finger even closer to his nose and said, "This is Martha's idea! She had to call it to my attention! She had to remind me that I have two children, not just one. She is so lovely, Fury, it was not said with criticism. It was as though all of us women were a group, but always watching out for our little ones and each other. It was as though Lil and Clay belonged to all of us, but you and I were their parents. I can't begin to imagine how we all managed till Martha became a part of our life. I don't even feel guilty or embarrassed – that would be a disservice to her concern. I just feel cross at myself for letting it get out of hand, so I'm going to go find Clay and bring him back to rest and relax."

She turned to go and Uncle Fury grabbed her around the waist, pulled her to him and said, "By the Gods, woman, you are even more beautiful when you're angry."

She tried to say, "F-F-Fury …"

But Uncle Fury planted one on her. (Clay told me that's what you say when people start kissin'.) I liked that, it made me feel like a big kid, then they just kissed real good and Uncle Fury let out a big sigh and said, "You and Martha are absolutely correct, my dear. May I suggest I go with you to bring Clay back? That way he won't lose his hard-won place in the sun, or his honor, or his pride. Also, if I'm there he can't be tagged as a 'Mama's boy'."

Oatie thought a moment then smiled at him, grabbed his arm and said, "Perfect, I'll run tell Martha we're on our way, then we'll not only relieve Clay, but I'll have a nice walk with my love."

I slid down the side of the tree where I'd been standin', watched Oatie come to Martha and whisper in her ear. They both smiled and she ran back to Uncle Fury.

Martha was puttin' the finishin' touches on somethin' she was makin' for the weddin'. She'd sent me to see if there was any hot tea for two little old ladies. Her eyes sparkled as she watched me understand her teasin'. I loved it and was still grinnin' when I got to the tree and saw Oatie and Uncle Fury. It held my attention and now I couldn't figure what to do. Should I still make my way to the cook fire, to tell Raff about the two little old ladies needin' tea or should I walk back to Martha ... I didn't even have to decide because Raff was headed towards Martha with two cups of tea.

I heard Raff say, "Where's Lil, should I just leave her tea? I don't want to it to get cold."

Martha interrupted her, nodded in my direction and continued foldin' up her handwork. She was grinnin'. I got to my feet and tried to remember the word Oatie had told me about. About somethin' I did. They weren't any of them mad at me, I just hadn't figured it all out yet. I didn't even know Martha knew I was behind that tree. I slowly walked towards the two of them. That tea smelled so good and when I reached them they were both watchin' me.

So I said, "I think I've been drippin' leaves again." They both looked startled and confused and it worried me. I didn't want any of 'em mad at me and so I looked at Raff, then at Martha and said, "You know, drippin' leaves, that thing Oatie says I do?" Still nothing. I really wanted to drink my tea, but it didn't seem like the right time. I struggled to remember everythin' Oatie had said, but all I could remember was, "Oatie told me I was a little pitcher – I don't know, are you mad? You're not sayin' anythin' to me ..."

I looked at Martha and she was shakin'. She pulled on Raft's skirt till she was sittin' down, still holdin' my cup of tea and they both started laughin'. They laughed and laughed and laughed and laughed. I just loved to laugh and I was wishin' they'd share with me, but they couldn't get their breath. I finally walked over to Oatie and got my tea.

I thanked her politely and said in as grownup talk as I could, "I wish I knew what was so funny, I like to laugh too, you know."

Raff leaned over, wiped eyes on her apron, pulled a hanky out of the pocket, blew her nose and said, "Oh-h-h-h, Lil."

That Martha was fannin' herself with her hanky and I guess they were gettin' over their, their, their fit!

Martha said, "Come sit with us a spell, darlin', and we'll try to explain why we got so tickled. Come on honey, climb up here." She patted the bench beside her. I put my tea down and climbed up beside Martha.

She patted me and Raff said, "Oh, oh, Martha, looks like we're facing a storm cloud here."

Martha looked down at me, put her arm around me and pulled me close. "We can shoo those storm clouds away. I think it's because our little one doesn't understand. Those are some pretty fancy terms she's dealing with. What do you think, Raff?"

"You know, Martha, our Lil is so smart and catches on to things so quickly that I think we often forget the enormity of all she's had to grasp, in a very short period of time. I fear we take her for granted many times."

Martha continued, "Lil, we were enjoying how your wonderful little mind deals with words that don't always make much sense to you, like 'eaves-dropping' and 'little pitchers have big ears.' You make everything fun, Lil, that's why we all love you so and everyone loves being around you. You're surrounded by happiness, my dear, so I guess everyone wants you for their very own."

I can almost get cross sometimes when I don't understand all that seems to be happenin' in my life. I don't understand all the words that go flyin' by me and what they mean. Everyone has different sounds to their voices when they talk, and with all the noise we live in here and the yellin' and new words, sometimes I want to cover my ears and get my pull cart and Miss Myrtle and Clay and run away deep into the forest where it's quiet and peaceful. But I've got responsibilities now, I'm growin' up and I have to take care of Martha and Billy Joe and Uncle Bear, Oatie and Raff, Uncle Fury and Miss Myrtle, Clay, and all my precious animals. I feel so sad at times because our life is so changed. There's great big buildings poppin' up everywhere my eyes can see. I know why I'm to stay with the wimmin by the cook fire, near our box house, because if I wandered away, I wouldn't never, ever find my way back. I think I want everyone to go home and leave us alone. I can't tell anyone how I feel, because everyone is workin' so hard and seem to be happy and it makes me feel terrible shel, selfish. The wimmin always makes my hurts better. I love 'em so much. I love my family and my new family and new friends, but there's too much, too many. I'm scared all the time that I'll take my nap and, when I wake up, I won't be in my box house in our bed, and I won't be able to find Miss Myrtle or Clay or my Mams and Uncle Fury, or Martha and Uncle Bear and … Billy Joe. I'll be alone again and … it makes me cold all over, and I'm scared, scared, bad scared.

My head was on Martha's lap and she was softly rubbin' my hair and I guess I drifted off, cause the next thing I heard was laughter and Clay's voice sayin', "Lil, wake up sleepyhead, let's you and me go to our secret place and hide and talk to each other. I'm so tired, and it sounds so good just to talk to you, let's do it. We can take a shawl and maybe Raff can bring us a couple of pillows. I'm so glad to be back to our home, Lil, and we just need to talk to each other. I missed you terribly and all of this made me so glad of how we were livin'. I know grownups know what's best, so I believe it's all goin' to be wonderful, but right now I'm tired and lonely. You can even bring Miss Myrtle if you want. I bet she's surely mixed up."

My heart about burst. I crawled off the bench and threw my arms around him. We just held each other. It felt so good. I saw Oatie slip away to the box house and I just knew she was goin' to get us shawls and pillows. Deep in my heart, I wished Miss Myrtle wasn't on vacation, but I knew it was for her protection and safety, but without Clay or Miss Myrtle, I couldn't have quiet secret talks and I was feelin' lonely too.

Clay and I turned as Oatie came up to us. She had a pillow and blanket in one arm and was draggin' my little pull cart. The other pillow and blanket was tucked into it and there, there layin' on top of 'em all tucked in was Miss Myrtle! I was suddenly so happy I burst into tears. I grabbed her up and held her so tight. Clay was cryin' too and didn't even care. He took the other blanket and pillow, put them in the pull cart, took my hand and we headed for our secret spot.

CHAPTER 2

Clay and I lost our home at the barn-raisin'. Oh, lots of wonderful things happened. It's all thrillin', excitin' and scary too. We've met great friends, but we've lost our precious little world. I've learned so much and it's made me grow-up. I long for the way it was and so does Clay. We're afraid we'll never, ever find any place again that is so beautiful, peaceful and quiet-like. All these new buildings are so raw. I do love the smell of the logs and fresh sawed wood, but it's just – just so big and empty and lonely somehow. We been talkin', and when all these loud happy folks leave, it will really be lonely and … scary. We don't feel happy with it, but we've made a pact that's like a promise, that we will keep our melons open to the change in our life and try really hard to see the good. It'll be hard, but he's right, it's our responsibility to our family and to the Wet Walkers that will be comin'. Oh my, there's almost too much for me and my melon.

    The happiest moments of every day are when that Runner comes trottin' up. He always comes to see me and tell me stories and make me laugh. He bounces up and down all the time he talks to me, then he blows me a kiss and off he goes. Clay and I both love him, he seems to understand we're gainin' a lot, but also what we are losin', somethin' precious. We will really miss him when this time is over.

But maybe he'll run up to see us ever so often. I told him that and he just laughed and laughed.

He said, "As a matter of fact, I'm needed to make a run to Middleboro to get some screws and nuts and bolts that's important for the end of all this buildin'. I'm ridin' my horse, though, cause I sure don't want to miss that weddin'! I have to admit I'll get to see Pokey, my little dog. I know she's missed her runs with me and I miss her more than I miss my Mother! Wish you could meet my little Pokey, Miss Lil, you two would be the best of friends. You ain't never seen a dog, but I'm here to tell you, you have a darlin' mare and Butter's a beauty, along with my pal Leggs and the sweet goats, but Miss Lil, if you've never had the love of a precious little dog, you ain't rightly lived."

He blew us a kiss and ran off.

I looked at Clay's sweet face. He was smilin', and I said, "Clay, did you have a dog? Are they all wonderful?"

Clay said, "Lil, they're a lot like people. Most are just the best, but sometimes they are not. Uncle Fury says if a dog is bad it's because it had a bad master. We had lots of dogs and I loved 'em. I-I-I wish we had dogs here. I really miss 'em. Uncle Fury says they're the only thing in the world who will love you totally – forever, in exchange for room and board."

There are five days left. That's all my fingers on one hand. I just love that. Each of my hands is full of five fingers. I wish everythin' was either five or ten. When I'm asked how old I'll be on my birthday, I hold up my one hand and say five, real proud. I can use both hands to tell 'em how old Clay will be. Five days to the weddin'. Whew, there's a lot to remember. Our new box home is ready. Clay says it looks like a castle. I didn't know what that was, but Martha told me stories about Kings and Queens in U-rup and princesses and princes.

She said, "Land sake, Lil, I'm gonna have to be careful about the stories I tell you. I'm afraid one of 'em will cause your eyes to pop right out of your head!"

I quick-like put my hands over my eyes so they couldn't get out, so they're safe for now, but I'm learnin' so much it's almost a worry.

This afternoon when the day's work is done, our two families are goin' to walk the property. I am so excited. We're goin' to see everything. We'll get to see our new home, our castle, and the most fun of all is Oatie's surprise. Uncle Fury had to make some decisions about our new home without Oatie. He's so scared she won't like everthin' that he's "sweatin' bullets," that means he's really fearful. I keep glancin' at him hopin' to see a bullet, but after Clay had a full on laughin' fit, he said not to waste my time. I haven't figured why people like to say things that are not what is ... but Clay just shrugged his shoulders and said he liked the sayin's, he thought they were lots more fun than just plain talk. It's just hard to figure. I'm tryin' to speak correctly and everyone else is changin' right talk into sayin's that sound different. Maybe 'stead of trying to talk right, I just need to say sayin's. I don't know, makes my melon sore.

Anyway, Clay says there's bunches and bunches of wagons sittin' up there, all covered up, just filled with furchur. That's too hard for me to say; so, we're callin' 'em "household goods." We've already got chairs and tables and beds and a rockin' chair. I don't see what else there could be or why we need anythin' else, but Clay just grins and says, "You'll see."

Our castle looks awful big tho, and I guess our household goods would fit in one little corner, so I'm guessin' it'll be a surprise for Oatie – and for me, too.

After today, she's not allowed to go in the house till after the weddin'. All these fine men will carry everythin' in and these dear hardworkin' wimmin will fix it up like it's supposed to be. Martha says it's the wimmins' duty to "make a nest." I just love that sayin'. It's like we're sweet little birds.

I heard Martha talkin' to Oatie and Raff about dear Runner. She was tellin' them about his life. She said he has the meanest mother that ever lived. His daddy ran off when Runner was just a little shaver, and she blames poor little Runner for that. She's so cruel to him that the whole town took him under their wings. It made my heart hurt to think anyone could be mean and cruel to that dear man. Everyone was surprised that he'd leave his little dog Pokey to come up here. Now they're all worried because he's not back yet and he was due last evenin'.

I told Clay what I'd heard and he hung his head. He said, "Not all Mams are like Oatie, Raff and Martha. I wish that wasn't so, but, Lil, it's true. My Mam was like that. I get aches in my stomach when I think of her. My dad was the best, 'course he was like Uncle Fury. Lil, do you know who reminds me of him? Billy Joe. Billy Joe is a lot like my pap was. Sometimes I see Uncle Fury watchin' him and seemin' like he's close to tears, and I'm thinkin' it's 'cause he's so much like Taylor, my father."

I'm worryin' about our little friend, and I know Clay is, too. I wish he'd pop up before we go on our walk, but we'll be goin' pretty soon. I need to help and I don't know how, and then I 'membered. I ran to find Raff. I found Raff and Martha standin' in the middle of the garden. Their arms was around each other and their heads was leanin' together. They must have heard me runnin'.

I was so out of breath when I reached 'em I could only blurt out, "Pray, Raff, please pray for Runner. We need to let God-Willin' know he's needin' help."

Both wimmin grabbed me and tried to calm me down. I had the gulps, but I got my story out and finally said, "I'm so worried and so's Clay and all the people too. Runner should have been back and he's not and I needed to do somethin', and all of a sudden I knew the only thing that could help was our God-Willin', and I knew I had to hurry and find you cause you know him better'n anyone and you could send him one of your prayers. Oh please, Raff, hurry. Somethin' might have happened to him."

Raff didn't hesitate, nor did she ask questions. She took Martha's and my hands, closed her eyes and tilted her head toward the sky. I knew I shouldn't be peekin', but I loved it so when she prayed and I kept thinkin' one of these times I'd catch a glance of God-Willin' a sittin' on her shoulder. When we said our Amens, I knew I'd done right to find Raff and get the message to God-Willin'. Seems like He must be real busy, but I know He always pays attention to Raff cause they seem to be awful good friends.

She said, "Thank you Lil, it's wonderful that you're so concerned for your friend, but it's even more wonderful that you've turned him over to God. Martha and I were just getting ready to round everyone up for our walk. Are you ready, Lil, to see all these miracles that God has provided for us? Let's go get our families together, shall we?"

We headed back to the box house and I skipped all the way. I knew Raff and Martha could admire the way my yellow shoes was hoppin' up and down as I skipped. I 'bout fell, I was makin' 'em jump so high.

Oatie and Clay was sittin' in front of the fire, talkin', and Uncle Fury, Billy Joe and Uncle Bear came 'round the side of the house, they were talkin' and laughin.'

Billy Joe was to be Fury's "best man," and Uncle Bear was givin' Oatie away, and Raff was the matron of honor, and Martha was a sort of Mother of the Bride, I forget the word, and Clay will carry the weddin' ring, and I will sprinkle flowers. Oh, I am so excited. I got real dizzy when they told me Uncle Bear was gonna give my Oatie Mam away. I got so scared I could hardly get my breath, but they all knew, so they reassured me over and over and explained the whole process till they were sure I understood it. Uncle Bear's just givin' her to Uncle Fury to love, and since I know he already does, it's all right with me.

When we looked at the storage between the old box house and the new box house, I couldn't believe my eyes. It had great big doors you could drive a wagon in and a reg'lar people door in one of the big doors in case you wasn't drivin' a wagon. There were small rooms in there and shelves and shelves and shelves. The whole back end was for wood storage. There was a doorway on one side and we walked in and out the other end. The whole thing was filled with wood with a big bin for chips and scraps. Course it was really full from all this building. Another big bin was filled with sawdust. Oatie reminded me how clean our property was and told me sawdust and brooms made that happen. It's also used in our garden to keep weeds from growin' and on and on. My eyes must have had that poppin' out look cause she took my hand and Uncle Fury took the other. He had Clay on the other side. That storage area was so good and I couldn't imagine ... then I remembered about good, better, best. My goodness, I've grown up. I'm so used to seeing good, better, best that I've almost forgotten how wonderful it is and how I felt when I was first learnin' to live.

We walked up the front steps to our new home. Oatie was streamin' tears, of course, but so was Uncle Fury, and Clay, and then I couldn't see good and found I was cryin' too. Our house had glass windows. The light twinkled and sparkled with the leftover sunlight and played on those windows and it was so beautiful. Now I knew why my little Mam had loved them so. They were all over this home and I was so glad.

Our front door had carvin's all over it, and I ran my fingers all up and down and around the carvings. I just loved it. It was beautiful. The rest of the house was flat wood and not very pretty, and I was about to ask Uncle Fury when I heard him tellin' Oatie that he had ordered bricks, but they couldn't get them till spring. Then bricklayers would come back up and cover our house with bricks. I didn't know how such a thing could be done. I looked at Clay and he was just beamin'.

He said, "Uncle Fury, is this like our ... our old home?"

Uncle Fury knelt down and wrapped his arms around Clay and hugged him hard. "Clay, this is just like the home you, your dad and I grew up in. It's a gift for you too, son, now let's show it to your new Mam and your new sister. How's that sound?"

Clay was cryin' hard and so was Oatie. I didn't understand anything that was goin' on, so I just decided to watch and listen. I knew one thing for sure – we'd passed clear over better and gotten to best real fast.

I didn't know what could be comin'. Uncle Fury opened the door, bowed, and with a sweep of his arms ushered us into our new house-home.

I learned what eyes look like when they are about to pop out. I'd never seen Oatie look like this. Her hands was coverin' her mouth, I guess so she wouldn't start screamin'. This was all too much for me. My whole family was actin' real crazy. This place was so big and there seemed to be more space in this house than there was in our whole world outside. All I could think of was, I'd get lost and they'd never find me. I felt awful cause I couldn't get excited like Clay and Oatie, but I was just scared.

I held on to Oatie's skirt till she'd finished huggin' and bawlin' all over Uncle Fury. She held on to his shirt flaps, looked into his eyes and said, "Fury, are-are-are we rich?"

Uncle Fury didn't even smile. He took her by the arms, looked right in her eyes, and said, "Oatie, with devilish hard work, fortuitous investing and God's blessing, we are very, very fortunate. I have pledged to God that if He indeed decided to bless me I would dedicate my life to the betterment of mankind. When I lost Taylor, it was as though it was a reminder of my promise. Will our good fortune make a difference in your feelings for me?"

Oatie gently put both of her arms around him and said, "Only to make me love you and your goodness more. Thank you, Fury, for everything. Thank you, Lord, may I be worthy of such a man."

I wanted to figger this all out, but I couldn't seem to bring it into a size that I could understand.

Oatie and Uncle Fury looked at me, and Uncle Fury said, "Is it too much, Lil? Does it make you want to go cover up your head in your old box bed?"

I loved 'em so much and I knew he'd done God's work and helped give us these miracles, and I wanted to be as happy and thrilled like everyone else, but I knew I was lettin' everyone down. I felt so bad and so lonely and cold in this big old place. What's wrong with me? Am I a bad child? Did these wonderful people end up with a bad child? Mebbe that's why my little Mam and Pap left me. Mebbe they knew somehow.

I looked at Clay and he was covered with sunshine. He was beamin', just beamin'. I'd never seen him look this happy – ever. He was grinnin' and sayin', "Home, it's home, oh thank you, Uncle Fury, thank you, thank you."

Mebbe God-Willin' would pick me up and take me to live with Him, because I didn't seem to like the new home He'd sent us. Tears ran so close to aspillin' over and I didn't want 'em to because I knew it'd be a gully washer. That's a sayin' that means too much water, and can wash you away. Everyone was lookin' at me, and I wanted to run.

All of a sudden strong arms swept me up, and I felt at home. Finally, I buried my head into my favorite good spot and breathed deep. I smelled his wonderful smell of trees and grass and leather, and smoke from a fire. He was hummin' softly and rockin' me back and forth. I felt so safe, and my gully washer didn't come. It was like when I was wishin' God would let me live with Him. He decided I needed to live right here – with my family, where He could keep an eye on me. I'd grow'd … grewn … grown up again and my insides was happy. I pulled my head up and put my finger on Uncle Fury's nose and my eyes looked into his eyes and I said, "I know I'll like our new house, Uncle Fury, but right now I just love my family and if you are gonna live here, then I want to live here too."

He hugged me so hard I could hardly breathe and I knew I was right. Wherever my family was, I wanted to be there, too. God had given me the best family in the world and He wouldn't have to keep remindin' me.

Clay was yankin' on my dress, sayin', "Get down, Lil, so's I can show you everything."

Uncle Fury said, "Clay, if it's all right with you, I think I'll just carry Lil through the first time, and then you can have a special private tour later, and you can share your good memories. How's that sound?"

Clay looked up at us and seemed to understand things. He and Uncle Fury looked at their eyes and Clay said, "I think that's a good idea, what do you think, Lil?"

I nodded. I felt fine, but I still had a bunch of shy lumps inside me, so I was lots happier bein' in Uncle Fury's arms.

Uncle Bear said, "Fury, if you start wearing out, I'll be glad to help you out carryin' Lil. She's growing up so fast she'll soon be too much for you." He was grinnin' that wonderful grin of his.

Billy Joe interrupted him and said, "Hey, do you two elderly gentlemen remember that she happens to be my girlfriend, my lady fair? When you two get tired, *I'll* take over."

Everyone was laughin' and I got to gigglin'. I thought to myself, I was Billy Joe's lady fair – oh I was so happy, but I still wrapped my arms around Uncle Fury's neck and stayed right in my safe spot.

It seemed like we were in that house forever. There was too much to see. There were two livin' rooms, both with their own fireplaces. A great big dinin' room with its very own fireplace. A kitchen that seemed as big as our box house with a great, great big fireplace. I loved that best.

Martha said, "Rocking chair in front of that fireplace will be wonderful for storytellin' time for little ones."

Oatie turned so red in her face I thought she must have something wrong with her.

Martha quick said, "Since I'm going to be a constant visitor, I'll have to request a rockin' chair, so Lil and I can have story time together as often as we like."

It all sounded wonderful, but the best part was where we were gonna eat our breakfast together. It looked out a big window into what was gonna be a herb garden. I didn't know what a herb was, but Raff really got excited.

Uncle Fury said, "I'm doing everything I can think of to convince you to move in with us, Raff." He grinned and said, "I think I've convinced Martha to stay with us."

Raff laughed and interrupted, saying, "She is not, she is staying with me – wherever I am."

Everyone laughed at that and Martha's sweet face was covered with smiles. She was gigglin' and said, "Now children, don't fight over me. However, I have to admit it does feel wonderful."

Uncle Bear said, "Harrumph, my dear, are you indicating that I wouldn't fight to the death for you?"

"And how about me, my darling Mother?" Billy Joe added.

Oh, this was so much fun. I was lovin' it.

The back porch was huge, and it walked down into a work yard where a cook fire would be. Off to the side was a dugout for a root cellar and a cold house. Clay's eyes got big, but he gulped and stood up tall and said, "Don't worry, Uncle Fury. I'm fine, just fine."

Uncle Fury ruffled his hair and turned and said, "And now, ladies and gentlemen – the *pièce de résistance*." I looked at him and he grinned at me and whispered, "That's French, darlin', and it means 'here comes the best part'."

My lands, there are too many best parts. I'm sure glad Uncle Fury is holdin' me cause I just might faint on the floor otherwise. Oatie and Raff explained to me a long time ago how that's what "ladies" did, when somethin' was too much for 'em. Then they'd have to sniff smellin' salts before they could sit up again. Oatie said "ladies" was delicate and genteel.

Raff snorted and said, "More'n likely, their corsets were too tight." They 'bout laughed themselves silly. I didn't know what on earth any of it meant or what a corset was, but I slapped my leg and laughed with 'em. That made 'em even laugh harder. Our family likes to laugh, and I'm sure glad cause it's my favorite thing.

We walked back to go see that *pièce* thing, and when we got to the dinin' room, Martha said, "Fury, what are those two big doors opposite the dining room for?"

Fury said, "Good grief, I must be overly excited. Billy Joe, would you open those doors?"

Billy Joe opened the doors wide and it was another room that just opened into the dining room.

Uncle Fury said, "This, my friends, is the music room. I plan to have dinner music every evening. We have two budding musicians in Lil and Clay and ever so many talented friends. If Martha teaches Lil to play the piano, then we'll have to think of some way to add a piano."

Now I'm excited. I am really excited. I must have gasped cause Uncle Fury looked at me and said, "Aha, do I detect a mighty twinkle in my little darlin's eyes?"

I loved it when he talked like that, and I turned his face to mine and kissed his nose three times. This was all such fun. Everyone seemed so thrilled, and I guess I was, too.

Martha said, "Lil darlin', can you manage steps?"

I couldn't think what she meant. She'd seen me go up and down our steps to our box house over and over. I can even hop up and down 'em. I was noddin' at her as we were walkin', and all of a sudden Uncle Fury stopped and turned me around.

I guess my mouth fell open and I thought I might be needin' those smellin' salts. This is what everyone had talked about. The house sittin' on top of a house. I was lookin' at more steps than I could ever imagine. I guess they was leadin' us up to that second house. They were held by a railing that seemed to curve around up to that 2-house. How in tarnation could I ever climb that many steps?

Uncle Fury said, "Lil, that's where our bedrooms are. What do you think?"

"Uncle Fury, I think it will be morn by the time I climb up all those just to go to bed."

Everyone laughed so hard and Uncle Fury danced around in a circle, with me hangin' on to his neck, and said, "Let's watch old Clay and see if he can make it."

I feared for poor Clay and quick said a prayer to God-Willin' to keep him from tumbling down those steps, all broken and dead.

Clay grinned at me and placed his hand on the banister (that's what that railin' is called) and he was up all those stairs before I could blink my eyes. I couldn't believe it! He was wavin' to everyone from the railin' up on that 2-house, and everybody was cheerin' and clappin'. He called down to me, "Don't worry Lil, I'll teach you how. It's easy and fun. I'll stay with you every time till you know how. You'll just love it, Lil, come on, everybody. You can see for miles."

Uncle Fury looked at my eyes and said, "May I carry you up the first time, Princess?"

Maybe I *was* a real Princess and this was our castle. I know if Clay could teach me to whistle, he could help me get up all these steps. I knew for sure I'd be sleepin' really well after gettin' up to my bed.

I nodded to Uncle Fury and said, "yes please," and up we went. It seemed so easy. We were at the top lookin' out the big beautiful window, and I was wonderin' at all I could see. I wondered if we could see Middleboro. Uncle Fury told me that it was too far for my eyes, but he pointed out the road that we'd ridden to say goodbye to Billy Joe, when I first heard about King. He turned around and I could look down into the foyay. I loved that fancy word. It just means where you come in to, but I like it fancy.

I said, "Uncle Fury, can I walk on my feet on this 2-house?"

He said, "Surely Lil, and if you want back up in my arms, just give a yank on my jacket. Does that sound all right?"

I nodded and he put me down right by Clay. Clay took ahold of my hand and all of a sudden all this big open space seemed glad we were there. I figured it was lonely for its family – and here we were. Clay and I went in every room. There were five bedrooms and a little parlor. He made me count 'em, and I got to hold up my five fingers. Uncle Fury's and Oatie's bedroom was bigger'n our box house. I asked why we all just couldn't sleep together in there and everybody got to talkin' at once, tellin' all sorts of reasons. Most of 'em didn't make much sense, so I stopped listenin'. They had a fireplace in their room and there was a little one in the parlor, too. My room and Clay's rooms and the other two were just empty boxes, but they assured me that would all change. I decided I'd just stop worryin' and look forward to all the new things that was happenin'. I was gettin' used to surprises.

Martha was sittin' on a bench-like box under a window in my room. I hadn't even noticed it. Uncle Bear and Billy Joe was askin' her if she was all right. She was pink in her cheeks, but she was pushin' at 'em and sayin' she was just fine. She spied me, patted the bench beside her, and said, "Oh Lil, you will love this window seat. You can sit here and look out at our wonderful world. Come, dear, and climb up here, so I can show you."

I hadn't even seen my window seat. I said, "Martha do you think they'll let me sleep on it so that I can look out at the stars at night?"

She said, "Oh Lil, that sounds so cozy. We'll have to beg and plead with Oatie, won't we?"

By the time we left our new 2-house, I was as excited as everyone else. It would never be lonely again. It would be filled with happy people who loved it. It would have its very own family, just like I do.

They let me walk down all those stairs, very slowly behind Clay, and I clutched the banister with all my might. Clay thought that was funny, but he didn't like me to be scared, so he said we should whistle our song "Tramp-Tramp-Tramp." That made it a happy adventure and when we got to the bottom, ever'body clapped.

Uncle Fury and Oatie came over to me and knelt down and said, "Are you all right, Lil?"

I told them in my biggety voice – that's what Raff calls it – "I most certainly am, and that was a grand adventure!"

We looked at those dear little Wet Walker cabins and I just loved them. They were small and cozy and each one had a wee fireplace of its very own. I knew then I was going to miss my box house. I had wanted Raff to come live with me in the 2-house, but now I'm glad she's stayin' in our box house. She must love it the same way I do. That makes my heart happy. We was walkin' two-by-two, and it was so much fun. Oatie and Fury was leadin' us, then Martha and Billy Joe, then Uncle Bear and Raff, then me and Clay.

I said, "Clay are you happy? Are we gonna be as happy as we were?"

He said, "Lil, I just don't know if we'll be as happy, but I know we'll be happy – maybe it'll be different, but I know we'll be happy. Don't you feel that way?"

"I know so many things, Clay, I worry some of 'em will fall out of my melon, but all this change scares me. I hated all these nice people coming here and makin' our life all different. Then I found out I liked all the people that I met. Then I hated that big house and it scared me. Then when we went inside everythin' changed again, and I just love 2-house. I didn't want all those Wet Walker cabins to take up all our pretty grassy areas, but now I've seen 'em and been in 'em. I think they're like our dear little box house. I know the poor people that's comin' will love 'em and their very own fireplace. I don't know nuthin', Clay, I mean – anythin'. Everythin' I thought would be fun was too big and too much, and now I'm likin' all of it. Is that the way it's supposed to be? Am I always gonna hate somethin' or ever'thin' and then end up lovin' it all?"

We were the last to cross over the stream and Clay helped me to the other side, stopped, smiled his sweet smile, and said, "Lil, I'm so proud to be your brother and your best friend, because you're exactly the way God-Willin' wants us all to be. He wants us to have an open mind." I gasped and my eyes got big.

Clay quickly said, "No, no Lil, that doesn't mean your seeds will fall out, it just means you're seein' both sides honestly, and then using good common sense to decide what's right for you. Uncle Fury would be so proud of you. He always tells me people don't use their heads, that they forget to think. He treasures good common sense."

Clay always made things better. He was so sweet and gentle and quiet, but he was always ready to laugh and have fun.

We looked up and could see Uncle Fury holdin' the gate for us. We ran towards him and I saw the biggest buildin' I'd ever seen. It was even bigger'n the house. I could hear my animals and that funny Leggs makin' all sorts of their noises, but I couldn't see 'em. It was a great big raw lookin' building, but Clay said, "It's going to be red, Lil. When spring comes, a bunch of friends will come back and they'll paint it red. We'll all help, and it will be so much fun. Everything else will be painted white, except for the doors of the cabins and the meeting/school/office house. All those doors will be painted red. Oatie and Raff's father and uncle were English and Irish. The doors to their little churches of England were always painted red. It meant welcome. Won't this be a pretty place, Lil, our home, won't it just be beautiful?" His eyes was, *were* just shinin'. I hoped mine were too, cause that's the way it made me feel, welcome.

That barn was so special. The animals had stalls and troughs to drink and eat out of. It smelled like new cut hay – and animals. It had a hayloft filled with hay rolls and even a tack room to keep saddles in. I wished sorely for my very own, but like Uncle Fury was when he was a boy – I had to be patient.

All that was left to see was the upper pasture where the tents were. They'd built a buildin' that could stable some horses, and keep some wagons safe and dry that belonged to the people travelin' west. We'd go see it and then we'd get ready for supper. All the fiddlers were gonna play and everyone could dance. They were usin' the spot still outlined in white rocks where the meetin' house would be, still empty for now. It was to be a hoedown – whatever that was. Guess I'll soon find out.

We'd about reached that last new buildin' when I heard awful sounds. Like an animal was screamin' somethin' worse. I looked at everyone to see if they'd heard it, too, and they had, they were all standin' rigid. All of a sudden, Uncle Fury, Uncle Bear, Billy Joe, Clay and a bunch of the workers started runnin' down the trail that we'd ridden our horses on.

I started to run too, but Oatie caught my arm and said in a fearful voice, "Lil, Lil no, darlin', you must stay with us. We don't know what this is, but someone or something is hurt. Badly. We'll wait here together till the men come back."

My heart was pounding and I was scared to death. All of a sudden I thought, "What if they never come back!?!"

CHAPTER 3

Oatie held tightly to my hand. Martha sat on a nearby log and Raff paced. We heard noises and ever so often we would hear that mournful cryin'. It was so awful I thought maybe that bad war had started agin and they was comin' to kill us.

Raff finally stopped pacin', looked at Oatie and said, "We may be needed."

Oatie nodded her head instantly and led me over to Martha. She leaned over and tilted my chin up so we could look at our eyes and said, "Lil, I want you to stay with Martha and see to her. <u>Do not</u> leave her for a minute. She is your responsibility and you are not to move from her side. Do you understand?"

I was noddin' my head so hard I was scared it'd fall off, but I wanted her to know I was big and I could take care of Martha. She waited till I climbed on the log and Martha put her arm 'round me, then she ran to Raff's side and they ran down the road. I sure hoped they was all gonna come back, cause if all that was left was me and Martha – well, seemed like we was a sorry lot.

All we heard were muffled voices from afar. I swore I thought I could hear feet runnin'. I looked at Martha and she said, "I hear 'em too, Lil, perhaps we'll know something in a minute. We best be very quiet."

All of a sudden around the far bend came about four or five men. Clay was in the lead and then a couple of the workers, who kept turnin' and lookin' behind them. Then came Billy Joe, carryin' something all wrapped up and a couple more fellas. Clay started hollerin' and whistlin' to the men and women from the tents who were waitin'.

"Dr. Wilkins, Dr. Wilkins, someone find Dr. Wilkins."

One of the men said, "He's in his tent, it's up near the high part. I'll go tell him you need him."

Clay didn't even slow down, he just kept yellin' and followin' the man.

I could hear someone yell, "Here! I'm Doc Wilkins, who needs me?"

The whole bunch crashed by us and headed up to the top of the upper pasture. We could hear 'em talk, but not many words. We figured they all went into the tent. We saw lanterns bein' lit, in his tent and all around, as other people lit theirs and went to his tent to help.

Martha wrapped her shawl around the two of us to ward off the chill of dusk. We just kept starin' down the trail. It seemed like it had been fearful quiet for a bit. I felt Martha gasp, but it was almost so soft that I felt it instead of hearin' it. I could see somethin' big comin' up the road. There was Oatie and Raff and Fury and other people. The big thing was my Uncle Bear. He was carryin' somethin' wrapped in a blanket.

I heard Martha mutter ever so quietly, "Oh dear God, please not …"

About that time Uncle Bear saw us and called out, "Martha dear, I'll be needin' you. Oatie will take Lil down to the cook fire to get the evening food fixed. You and Raff and Fury can be a help to me if you will. We'll put off tonight's festivities till tomorrow night. I'm sure everyone will understand, tomorrow being Friday, and two days before the weddin'. Means the pastor and his wife and family will all be here. It'll be better and for our little feller too."

Uncle Bear never stopped walkin', his big boomin' voice was just a talkin' to Martha.

She was sobbin' and could only say, "William, is it Runner? Is he, is he …"

"Yes Dear, it's Runner, he's bad right now, but I think he's going to be all right, we're all gonna be with this little feller till he is all right. Mark my words."

Oatie broke off and came to us. She kissed Martha and said, "He'll be needin' your lovin' touch, Martha. He finally recognized William and asked for you."

A sob caught in Martha's throat as she leaned down and kissed me. She said, "Go with Oatie and help her, darlin', we'll be down as soon as we can."

I nodded and said, "Martha, if Runner' s sick or hurt, will you remind him that Lil and Clay loves him a whole lot?" I looked at Oatie real quick to see if I said it right. Her lips was in a straight line, but her eyes smiled at me. She picked me up and carried me towards the box house, as Martha hurried towards William's tent.

Oatie seemed so quiet that I just couldn't make myself ask her all the questions I needed answers to. She almost looked like she was walkin' in her sleep. My melon was so full of questions that I know it was close to burstin', but I still couldn't ask her.

I'd never rightly met anyone like Runner. He was so kind and so happy. What could have happened to him to hurt him so? Was he going to die? Maybe he lost an arm or a leg and didn't know where to find it. I wasn't a bit hungry, and Oatie didn't seem like she cared a whit for fixin' food. I bet she's not hungry either. It was dark now, and no one had come down for dinner yet. All of a sudden I knew what I wanted. I wanted to put my nightie on, get Miss Myrtle and climb into our big cozy bed. Maybe I could put my melon to sleep instead of ruinin' this good day with this bad endin'.

I told Oatie what I wanted to do, and she just looked at me for a bit. Then she said, "Really, Lil? Do you really want to go to bed? Are you sure you don't even want a bread and butter sandwich or a glass of milk?" I shook my head and said I wanted the bad part to go away.

She sighed and said, "I'll come in in a few minutes and help you get ready for bed."

I said, "Oatie, if I'm big enough to watch over Martha, and that was my first time – then I'm big enough to get ready for bed by myself. I almost do that by myself every night. I'm just sleepyheaded. I can stay and keep you company if you'd like."

Oatie finally smiled with her mouth. It wasn't enough to scare clouds away, but she seemed comfy enough to let me go.

My beloved dark night put its arms around me and helped me let go of my scary thoughts. The fire was low and seemed to be tellin' me we'd all be fine. I wasn't likin' this dyin' bit. All I knew about it was, you went to live with God-Willin' and that was good, but you wouldn't see the person again and that was bad. I closed my eyes, and since I knew Miss Myrtle was already asleep, I had no one to talk to so I guessed I'd just go to sleep too. Everyone in my family had been sheddin' tears 'cept me. Maybe I'd already cried so much that I'd used 'em all up. I would surely miss 'em.

It seemed like I was extra warm and cozy, so I opened my eyes a little. I knew it wasn't morn, but the fire was bigger and I could see bigger movin' shadows. Was I havin' that dream again? Was I lost and couldn't find my family? I felt for Miss Myrtle, and she was right beside me, so we must still be in our bed. One of the shadows moved the rocker closer to the fire and then I could see it was my three Mams. I could tell they hadn't been to bed, cause they still had on their yesterday's clothes. They was whisperin' to each other and they kept glancin' my way to see if they'd waked me. I had pillows and covers all piled around me, and I could just barely see 'em, and I couldn't hear 'em at all. I finally figured that if I wanted to know what happened, I'd have to let 'em know I was awake. I wanted to know so badly, but if it was real bad, then I don't think I wanted to know at all.

I was amullin' on this when I became aware of a shadow above me. It was Raff. She was pattin' the top of my head and shushin' me.

She said, "Lil, I know you're awake, darlin'. Come, let me wrap this shawl around you and I'll carry you over to the fireplace. You need to know what all is happenin'. We weren't shuttin' you out, sweet dear, but for a while so much was up in the air …"

I tucked Miss Myrtle under the covers and held my arms up to Raff. Her strong arms picked me up like I was a little cloud, wrapped me up and, before I knew it, us four wimmin was sittin' in front of our happy dancin' fire. They all had a cup of tea and there perched in front of the fireplace where it'd stay warm was another cup for me! I was so thrilled. Whew, this must mean I'm really grow'd up and important too. Raff picked up my tea and I wrapped my hands around it.

Raff said, "Will you be able to hold it all right, Lil? I put it in a mug so you could hold on to a handle."

I nodded as hard as I could without spillin' it.

She went on. "This has been a sad evenin', Lil, and it has changed the directions in people's lives. We have decided that Runner will be livin' permanently with us. One of the little cabins will be his, will be his home. He will be our responsibility, and we will provide him with love and security and a family till he no longer needs us. In other words, I suspect he'll be with us for the rest of his life. We felt you would be happy about that, so it's a family decision. We want you to feel that you have a say in it, so if for any reason you don't feel good about this, please say so."

They were all lookin' at me with serious faces and I felt so proud. I felt good inside, and I said, "He can live with us and we can keep him safe."

Raff kissed the top of my head and said, "God-Willin' will keep him safe, but we will keep him happy. He loves Martha so, we weren't sure he'd stay up here. William and Martha were willing to take him right into their home but, well, Martha's not always feelin' wonderful, and she and William and Billy Joe will be up here so much that, well, it just worked out fine. Martha's worn out from holdin' his hand. His happiness seems to depend largely on Martha, and luckily you and Clay … and of course …"

"Pokey," Martha said. "If only Pokey …"

Oatie spoke up quietly, but firmly, and said, "Pokey is going to make it. She knows how much Runner needs her and she wouldn't let him down. We need to pray for the healing of both of them." She sighed heavily.

I wasn't gettin' my puzzle fixed. I didn't have all the pieces. I could do the puzzles that they made me an' Clay pretty good, but they always told me you can't ever solve a puzzle if you don't have all the pieces. Clay and I both knew puzzles, and how to solve them was a bigger teachin' than just a game. I said, "Will Runner be our brother?"

They all looked like they hadn't thought of that.

Raff said, "Oh Lil, you and that melon of yours!" She went on, "Not exactly. In God's eyes we're all part of a family, His family, so we have just asked Runner to be a part of our little family. Our family has extended to include Martha, William and Billy Joe and now ... Runner. Does that feel right to you, Lil?"

I nodded big and answered, "An' our animals, an' ... Pokey."

They all seemed relaxed and happier. I guess they'd got everyone fed and sent off for a good night's rest. The next two days would be filled to the brim. They were all chattin' and plannin' and remindin' me that the Pastor and his wife and kids would be comin' tomorrow, and the next day was the weddin'.

I waited for a pause in the chatter and I said, "Will the Pastor's children be littler than me?" They all looked at me funny.

"Littler than you?" Oatie said, and looked at Martha and Raff.

They looked back at me and Martha said, "Well, Lil, now that you mention it, I don't believe any of their children are littler than you. I believe the youngest one is nine. Dear child, that's an interesting question. Does it worry you that you're the littlest angel that we have?" Martha had a way of makin' everybody feel better. She had just called me their littlest angel.

Somehow my worry about bein' the littlest forever wasn't quite so worrisome. I said, "I never seen anyone littler than me, and I keep thinkin' how much fun it would be to have someone littler to take care of. Clay says it makes him so happy to have a little sister and a little friend. I-I-I guess I'd just like to have one too."

They were all lookin' at me with smilin' faces and I thought, now is the time,

I said, "Can you tell me what happened that hurt Runner and Pokey?"

They looked at each other and Martha said, "Lil, dear, it's actually a very long story that began many years ago, but I'll try to tell you the jist of it. Runner must be at least forty years old. We didn't think much of his folks. They were both, well, just downright mean. I don't think he ever had love from anybody. Didn't seem to affect him for some reason. He just seemed to love everybody and be happy. He was but a babe when his Daddy ran off. We all thought maybe it would make his Mama nicer, you know – like his Pa was the problem! Well his Mama just got meaner. She wasn't good at anything and mean as a snake to boot, but the townspeople tried to help her make a livin'. We all took turns with Runner and, God love him, he was worth every minute we gave him. His Mama went from house to house doing little menial chores and complainin' all the time and even stealin' bits and pieces from the households." She shivered, "Terrible woman. Well when he was between four and five, he was always tryin' to help everybody and we decided he'd be the town errand boy. He was thrilled and became a part of all of our hearts and homes. That wicked women charged us all the highest rate she could for his upkeep. We knew differently. We kept him in clothes, fed him, saw that he bathed, took him to the doctor, and saw to his schoolin' and church. She never gave him a penny for his own. He's been a wonderful part of our lives for about thirty-five years or so, and it will be a hardship for the folks to find he'll no longer be there."

Martha paused and thought for a minute. Then she said, "A tinker came through town one day about three years ago, and he had a sweet little dog and a little pup. He said she'd had four, but he'd managed to find homes for all of them except this little one. She seemed to be too gentle and shy and too content with nothing. He told us most folks preferred their little dogs to have a lot of spunk, but this little dog was, well, just Pokey. We gave the man a little money and put Pokey in a little basket near the stove. It was our time to feed Runner, so when he came in after his errands were done, we told him we had a present for him. I remember the look on his face. He was so excited he bounced up and down in a circle instead of just up and down. We led him over to the stove and raised the little cover, and that little dog looked up at him, and our Runner was never the same. Happiness knows no bounds, you know. It was the sweetest love I've ever witnessed. All Runner could say was, 'Aw-w-w-w, Aw-aw-w-w,' over and over, tears gushin' out of his eyes. He quietly sat down without twitchin' and bouncin', just sat right down on the floor, cryin' and sayin' 'aw-w-w-w.' That little pup crept out of its little basket and went to Runner and curled up on his lap, sighed a contented little sigh, and went to sleep. I spoon fed Runner some soup and biscuits because he wouldn't move away from that pup! We made him a pallet to sleep on near the stove, and Pokey slept the night in his arms. Coming up here is the first time he left her. Unfortunately, he left her with his Mother. We don't know what-all has happened, but Runner and Pokey were both bleeding and had been hurt. Pokey was so still, we all thought she was dead, but she feebly licked my hand when I scratched her chin. We can't imagine what all that woman did, beside hittin' him with a shovel over and over and callin' him a freak.

"He clutched my hand, Lil, and finally said, 'Miss Martha, I'm not a freak, am I?' William answered him in that powerful voice of his that makes us all think he's God and said, 'Listen up, Runner. You're not a freak, you're the best friend we have, and you and Pokey are going to be just fine. We're thinking Fury and Oatie and Raff and Lil and Clay will be needin' so much help that maybe you'd consider livin' up here with them. Miss Martha will be up here a lot, and Billy Joe and I will be comin' up to help 'em every other weekend.'"

Martha went on, "Can you imagine that, Lil?" She was gigglin' and afore long, we were all laughin' and nothin' was scary any more. She said, "As soon as he heard William and knew little Pokey was gonna live, he let go, and I feel all the tears he shed were tears of relief and gratitude.

"Dr. Wilkins says not to worry, Pokey is under control and is just missin' Runner. We're going to bring her to him this afternoon, and maybe you and Clay can check on them? His soul has been trampled on, Lil, and that hurts worse than any pain he endured from his Mother's beating. We must love and nurture them, but I know in my heart with them livin' up here, this story will have a happy ending."

I felt so bad and so good that I hugged and kissed Raff, slid off of her lap and went to Martha. I gave her big hugs and kisses and thanked her for fixin' my puzzle, then I went to Oatie. I looked at her eyes and said, "Mam, would you tuck me in my bed? I want to go to sleep now, because I've got all the makin's for good dreams in my head."

Tears streamed out of Oatie's eyes, of course, but she picked me up and carried me to the bed. My arms was around her neck and I nuzzled her.

She said, "I love you, Lil,"

I said, "I love you, too, and I love Raff and Martha and ever'body in our family, but I'm so glad you're my Mam."

CHAPTER 4

It's Saturday morn, it's Saturday morn, oh what a happy day! I ran to the door and looked out. That big old sun was comin' up and it was so beautiful. The sun was poring through the lacy ferns and makin' starry shadows ever'where they fell. Our land was covered with lace filled with the sparkles from the morning dew. Oh, how I loved our home and our land. Oatie says when you first greet the mornin', stand tall and take deep breaths and fill your lungs with that brand new untouched fresh, fresh air. I did it over and over, and it was so good.

I opened the door wide to see if everyone was gone. I bet they went to take care of Runner. I ran back to the bed and started my mornin' routine so's I could go see him too. I stopped still. It was surely quiet ever'where. I was goin' as fast as I could go. I was tryin' to get my day figured out.

The folks are movin' Oatie and Fury, my Mam and Pap. That gave me a big lump in my throat. Yep, they are my Mam and my Pap – and Clay's. Everyone else is part of our family, but they are our Mother and Father. I'd never said those words out loud, and they felt strange to me.

Oatie, no, my Mam, had put out a soft flannel shirt and clean overalls. The shirt was my favorite, because it was the blue striped one that matched my eyes. I bounced out of the house and looked around me. I didn't see anyone anywhere. I decided instead of racin' pell-mell, I'd try to be ladylike. I knew all the Mams would like that.

When I walked around to tent town, there was people walkin' around quiet like. Clay came out of William's tent and his face was beamin' and happy. He saw me and waved and come runnin' over to me, grabbed me by the hands and jiggled me around in our dance – without sayin' a word.

I didn't know what to think. I said, "Clay, what's wrong? Why is ever'body so quiet? Why aren't the folks talkin'? Is Runner all right? What about Pokey?"

Clay grinned great big and said, "Everyone's fine, Lil, people are trying not to make much noise so Dr. Wilkins' patients and Runner can rest and not get too excited. Our Mam and Pap have a surprise for you, but I can't tell it. Oh Lil, I wish they'd hurry.

"All the folks are getting ready to pull the wagons down the back way to 2-house and start moving the 2-household goods in. Runner is so happy he's gonna live up here with us and be part of our family, and he wants to get up and go help move the pieces into the house, but Dr. Wilkins won't let him. The wedding practice is this afternoon and I'm excited. There's almost too much happening today. The Pastor will be here with the rest of their kids by lunchtime. They're all red-headed and freckled. Margaret Fay has made Oatie, I mean our Mam's weddin' dress almost all over from scratch. Our Mam is so thrilled her eyes haven't stopped dancin'. I've decided to call Uncle Fury Father. He likes it, says it makes him feel important. He called his Pa Father and his Mam Mother. What do you think we should do, Lil? Do you like the words Mother and Father?"

"Clay I swan', I think I'm goin' back to bed. I can't keep up with your jabberin'. I'm tryin' to act real ladylike, but it's not much fun. I'll be glad when we can be ourselves and laugh out loud. I want to go see Runner, and I sure want to see that Pokey. Can I do that yet?"

Clay said, "Well you probably can't right now, at least not till Oatie and Fury, I mean, Mother and Father come out."

I looked at Clay and said Mother and Father a few times under my breath. It really sounded pretty when Clay said that. I think I'll feel goofy at first, but I'm gonna try, cause with all the changes that will be happenin' to us, I want to do the very best things that will make them and us the happiest.

"Clay, there's our Mother and Martha comin' out, can I go ask her about my surprise and seein' Runner and Pokey?"

"Lands no, Lil, she'll have me by my ear! It's supposed to be secret and a surprise. I shouldn't have said anything, but that's not a good reason and she and Father would be disappointed in me. Golly, it sure sounds hard to say Father – but we'll get used to it. Here they come. Lil, please don't tell them that I can't keep a secret."

Oatie, I mean Mother, held her arms out to me and I ran into them as fast as I could. She swept me up and kissed me all over. "You did a good job of washin', Lil. You smell clean and sweet."

Martha said, "Oatie, let me have a little time so I can smell that clean sweet child."

Oatie, I mean Mother, set me down and I buried my head in Martha's skirts. Oh, I hope I grow up and smell like Martha. I'll never forget her smell. It's fields and flowers and the sweetness from our land. It's just "my Martha." Mother ran back to the tent and came back with Father. They were both grinnin' mighty big.

Martha giggled and said, "Oh, Oh, Lil, looks like something special is coming your way."

I turned round and leaned backward into Martha's skirts. She put her arms down over my shoulders. Mother and Father knelt down to look in my eyes.

Unc-Father said, "Clay says you'd like to go see Runner and Pokey. Is that so?"

I said, "Oh yes, please, thank you, please yes."

I couldn't seem to keep my polite words straight but they had their minds on something else. They said, "You must be very, very quiet because we're trying to keep him – them – all quiet." They each had ahold of my hands. I was almost scared.

When they opened the tent door, my Uncle Bear was all I could see. He was watchin' Raff spoon soup into little Runner's mouth. He turned and gave me a hug and a kiss and said, "Runner, looks like you have company. Are you ready?"

"I sure am, Oh Miss Lil, you get to meet my Pokey. Oh thank you for comin' to see me. I'll be up and around in no time."

I got me a big case of shy lumps. One of his eyes was covered in bandages and the other one was all black. He had awful lookin' cuts all over his face and arm. His other arm was all in bandages too and it all scared me. I'd never seen anybody hurt so much. I was pullin' back a little.

But Unc-Father said, "Come here, Lil, and meet our Miss Pokey – she's our miracle dog."

I wanted to run from the tent. I didn't want to see Runner hurt, and I was scared to see a dog. What if it decided it wanted to eat me all up? I started wailin'. Unc-Father picked me up and rubbed my back and shushed me and said very quietly, "Lil, you must be very, very brave, and try not to cry. You see, Runner doesn't know how scary he looks. He has been terribly hurt and has been told he's a freak. We must be extra gentle and kind so that his poor heart will heal. Can you do that for me and your family who loves you, but especially for Runner and Pokey? Can you do that, love? Can you be a very brave big girl so that we don't make him feel worse?"

I gulped and gulped and finally turned my Father's head around. I put my finger on his nose and said, "I'm very, very brave, Father, please put me down, but come with me, don't leave me."

He said, "I'll be right here, Lil, whenever you need me."

I walked over to the cot and patted Runner's good arm. I said, "Lan' sakes, Runner, you 'bout scared us all to pieces. I'm so sorry you're hurt, but I sure am happy you're gonna live with us."

His little bony face broke into a crooked sore lookin' little smile. He said, "Thanks Lil, I'll be a big help to you all, and to you and Clay. Come see Pokey. She's layin' in her box with her pups. One of them is yours and one is to be Clay's. He says you're to have first choosin'."

I looked up at Father and held my arms up. He swung me up, and I finally saw the box. I didn't have any idea what to look for, and I didn't know what all this meant. Father walked me to the box and knelt down and put me on his knees so I could look into the box. There lay the prettiest little animal I'd ever seen. She was golden with silky hair and long ears. She had great big velvet brown eyes and a little pink nose.

I squealed and said, "Uncle Fury, help her! They's rats eatin' her, help her, help her!" I was tryin' to climb up in his arms so they wouldn't get me.

He said, "Lil, Lil, calm down, honey. Those are her precious little pups and they are havin' their breakfast right now. Pokey's a good mother and she's mighty proud of her puppies. This is God-Willin' workin' with the animal kingdom, Lil. It's a beautiful thing. He's allowing this dear little dog to feed her babies until they are big enough to eat real food, then she'll wean them and they'll be on their way to being the cutest little dogs you've ever seen."

I was not convinced of anythin' he was sayin', and I didn't understand half of it.

He said, "We've decided you and Clay need little pets. That way Pokey will be around her little girls and they needn't be separated. How's that sound, Lil?"

I was so afraid I was going to disappoint everyone, but I was sure I was about to either bawl or be sick, maybe both. I forced myself to look down in that box again, and that little dog's big brown eyes were fixed on mine. It was as though she knew what I was feelin' and it broke her heart. I was so ashamed I didn't know what to do. I looked up at Uncle Fury, oh my, I mean Father, and then back down at Pokey's eyes and I said, "May I touch her?"

My Father said, "I think she wants you to, Lil, pat her little silky ears and scratch her chin a little."

I was so scared I thought surely I would die right there, but I put my hand on her little ear. It was so soft I was surprised. It was the same size as my hand. I patted it again and then I scratched real easy under her chin. She looked at my eyes and stuck her little tongue out and rubbed it on my hand. It was a kiss. I knew it and I knew she saw I was scared, and she was tryin' to tell me it was all right. I loved her. I felt awful bad cause her babies was so ugly, but I vowed to her silently that I would try to think they weren't ugly and I'd really try to love 'em.

CHAPTER 5

I touched that sweet little dog again and felt her silky ear between my fingers. I whispered to her that it would be all right. Lookin' at her little rats, I didn't know how it could be, but I wasn't goin' to be the one to tell her that her rats was ugly. Poor thing. She never took her eyes off of me and she kissed me over and over with her poor little rough tongue. I wish I could have her instead of her little rat, but since I was doin' better and was very brave, it *would* be better and I'd never let her know.

I felt some jostlin' and I was hopin' Uncle Fury was, I mean, my Father was goin' to carry me out of that bad room, but it was Clay. He had tiptoed in and was just a beamin'. I figured he hadn't seen 'em yet. Oh, what if he hollered when he saw 'em, poor little Pokey'd know.

I quickly said, "She's been lickin' my hand, Clay. She's the dearest little dog, I just love her." (I'd get his mind off the rats and when he realized those rats are our surprise he won't be so upset.)

He said, "Oh Lil, I know, she's a wonderful dog, the best really, but look at her pups!"

Oh no, Clay, don't get upset, everyone will feel awful. Oh what can I say? Why won't he look at me and understand that we have to pretend to be excited. He's jabberin' and sayin' terrible things, he's even ticklin' one of the rat's tummies. What's wrong with him, doesn't he know nuthin', I mean, anythin'?

He said, "Oh Lil, have you ever seen anything as precious as her pups? Look how full their little tummies are. Look Lil, they're all full of milk and are gonna go to sleep. Oh, how I wish we could pick 'em up, but we're not allowed to handle 'em for a few days till they're stronger. Oh, I can hardly wait. Have you thought about which one you'll choose? Have you picked out a name yet?"

I didn't rightly know what to think or what to do. Poor Clay has turned into an idjit. I wish I could do that lady thing and just pass out on the ground. A name? What's wrong with him? I guess we could call 'em Ugly1 and Ugly2. Has everybody taken leave of their senses? I know when I tell Miss Myrtle, she'll have a vapor fit. She won't want no, *any* dog that looks like that a livin' in our house with us.

Clay was lookin' at me funny. He said, "Lil, don't look so sad, the days will pass fast and then we can hold 'em. See, their eyes aren't open yet. They're blind and fragile. Oh Lil, don't cry. We'll soon be able to hold 'em and love 'em, you'll see. Won't we Uncle – I mean Father?"

Unc-Father leaned down and picked me up and said, "C'mon, Clay, let's let these patients rest and catch up on their strength. You and Lil can come back this evening again to see them all. Just don't stay long – all right?"

Clay nodded and I tried to think of something to say. I couldn't, so I just held on to my Father's neck as tight as I could. Well, this is a fine kettle of fish, that's a sayin'. It means a mess, and that's sure right! My big surprise! A blind rat! Wait till I tell Miss Myrtle.

I waved at poor Runner as we went out. He looked tired and sick, but happy. I was guessin' he hadn't seen 'em yet, and he felt fine, cause he knew he could get rid of 'em by givin' 'em to two little kids. It was hard for me to think of Runner bein' anythin' but kind and good, so I must try to understand. I guess Oatie's been too busy to see 'em yet. I sure hope she doesn't, it would surely ruin her weddin' day!

Father was carryin' me and holdin' Clay's hand. Clay was jabberin' lickety-split and was still talkin' about our surprise. I buried my head in my favorite spot so I couldn't hear him.

Father turned his head into my curls and kissed me and said, "You're mighty quiet, little girl. It's been quite a morning. Let's see if your Mother will let you ring that dinner bell so that the workers can have some breakfast before their hard day. How does that sound?"

I kept my head buried, but I nodded hard so he'd know I was thrilled. Clay was still jabberin', and I didn't know how to make him shut up, so I just kept thinkin' about the bell. Father stood me down right by the fire and it felt wonderful. I hadn't known how cold I was.

Martha started rubbin' my hands with her warm ones and said, "Clay, run get Lil's sweater before she turns into a stick of ice. She won't be able to ring the bell if she's so cold she can't move."

Clay scampered towards the house and Martha and I stood close to the fire.

Oatie, my Mother, said that Margaret Faye could tend to the next shift with Runner, till we all met here for the rehearsal. Then one of her sons would take over. I was warm now, and I had my sweater on. I clanged the bell and it was really fun. I clanged it agin and all the people trailin' in and out of the new box house, our 2-house, came hoppin' down to eat their grits and hot bread and bacon. They were laughin' and talkin' and in a minute our whole yard was filled. I'd never seen the whole bunch together, because they'd been eatin' up by the fire at the tent town. Raff had decided it would be easier on Runner if they kept their noise down here. It was really fun for me to watch 'em. There were big boys and girls, but out of all of 'em, Clay and Roy Jack were closest to being little like me. Roy Jack was almost eleven, but he wasn't taller. Clay would soon be ten, and they were a lot of fun to watch and listen to. Course, they started talkin' about those rats, and I lost interest and snuggled close to Martha. I was wishin' I could go back to bed with Miss Myrtle and start this day over, but that wasn't going to be. I was in a sour way, and I didn't know what to do to make it better.

Martha said, "Lil, are you gonna play some music at the hoedown tonight?"

That perked me up and I said, "Martha, I haven't practiced very much. I don't want to play unless it sounds good."

Martha said, "Why Lil, practice in your head, dear. Close your eyes and go through your songs in your head. I played for church for years and I practiced for real as much as I could and the rest of the time I'd practice in my head. By the time Sunday came, I could almost play everything with my eyes closed. You'll see. It's as much fun as practicing."

I loved Martha, she made everything happy and better. I was wonderin' if she could maybe fix Uglyl and Ugly2, but I didn't want to upset her or ruin her day.

The folks was finishin' up and scrapin' their plates into the "chicken bucket" and headin' back to work. I wished I could go watch 'em, but we all needed to have a last fittin' on our wedding clothes. Then the rehearsal, then dinner, then the hoedown. It all seemed a lot and I couldn't help it. I yawned a big yawn.

Martha giggled and said, "Lil, you're worn out. I think you need a wee nap right after the rehearsal and then you'll be filled with energy. It would be terrible if you turned into a sleepyhead in the middle of your music and fell in a heap on the ground and started snoring."

We laughed and laughed and my sour feelin' was gettin' better. She made me a snuggle place on her lap and started singin'. I lay my head down and just listened. Oatie, my Mother, chimed in and those two could sing the birds outta the trees. That's another sayin' that tells how good they are.

Clay's sure right – those sayin's are more fun than talkin' right. That "talkin' right" makes you worry, but sayin's seem to say happy things and make people laugh. When Martha pats my head and sings, I swear it just makes me sle-e-e-epy.

The Wet Walkers

I woke up hearin' Uncle Bear and Father laughin' about something. There seemed to be so much talkin' from the folks fixin' 2-house and the rest that had gathered that I knew I couldn't have barely closed my eyes. I sat up and rubbed 'em good so they could see and looked at Martha.

Her eyes was just twinklin' and she said, "Well, little darlin', we surely got that nap out of the way. I think you ought to be ready to face the whole evening. What do you think?"

I said, "Martha, do I get heavy when I sleep on your lap? I never mean to go to sleep, but I'm thinkin' it must be my favorite place cuz I sure do it a lot. Listenin' to you sing is almost better than sleepin' in my bed."

Martha just smiled and hugged me close. She said, "You're light as a little feather, Lil. Seems like I always manage to slip a few winks in myself." We all laughed and I thought, see there, how much fun that sayin' was? I'm not quite sure of the winkin' bit yet, but I'll get it figgered and add it to my other ones.

The "wedding party" had gathered and even Margaret Faye and her husband the preacher was here, so I guess we were about to start. I was excited and so was Clay. He came over, kissed Martha, grabbed my hand and sat down. Margaret Faye was tellin' everybody all sorts of things, like where they started from and when and where we all needed to stand. There were three men with fiddles and two of the bigger boys with gee-tars. We was gonna walk into the garden while they played music. That preacher was gonna walk first and stand in the circle where the lacy carrot tops had been and THEN Raff would walk into the garden and stand on the other side, THEN Clay would walk in and he'd be carryin' the pillows Martha had made that would have two rings tied on them with little ribbons. Just thinkin' about all of this prettiness excited me, and I could hardly keep from jumpin' up and down.

THEN it was my turn, right after Clay, and I was gonna carry a little basket Martha had made. It was covered in pretty silky coverin's and trimmed with ruffles and lace. There weren't many flowers bloomin' right now, but they'd made bows out of silk ribbons and they'd also found some ro-do-dren bushes that had soft white petals. I got to sprinkle the ribbon bows and petals on the ground and my Mother and Uncle Bear would walk on 'em. My head was dizzy. I was so thrilled. My Uncle Bear was gonna give my Mother to my Father and we was all goin' to see it and make sure they did it right!

We did it three whole times and I just loved it. I wanted to keep on doin' it, but Margaret Faye laughed and said we needed to go in the box house cause that's where all the weddin' finery was. The men's finery was in 2-house, and I guess that dear little Runner had brought a lot of extra important items, and the preacher had brought all the men's weddin' clothes.

We had candles lit all over in our little box house and since it was still light outside, it was all soft and beautiful. One of the older girls was perched at our front door keepin' it open for extra light and keepin' any nosy bodies out. Margaret Faye had taken over sewin' the dress that Oatie and Raff had been makin', and I don't ever 'spect to see anythin' so beautiful. It fit her just right and then Martha unwrapped a lacy collar that was called a "bertha." She had worn it at her own wedding to Uncle Bear, and Oatie was to wear it, cause you're suppose to wear "somethin' old and somthin' new, somethin' borrowed and somethin' blue." It was what wimmin did at weddings, and it was for good luck, so they was important. So Martha's "bertha" was somethin' borrowed and somethin' old. Raff put her blue ring on Oatie's other hand, and we was all in a tizzy because we didn't really have anythin' new. I was startin' to feelin' sad because that meant Oatie, I mean my Mother and Father, wouldn't be havin' good luck.

The girl guardin' the door left her chair and walked down the steps. She was talkin' to someone. See, I thought, that bad luck thing was already startin', cause we didn't have anyone guardin' the door. I'd never figgered what she was guardin', but it must be important. I knew she was one of Margaret Faye's children, because she had red hair and freckles. Her hair was bright red and she wore it in two thick braids. She was sixteen and was always nice to me. She smiled a lot and she had "spectacles." I'd never seen such before and she told me she didn't see very well without them. I couldn't think why, cause she had two eyes just like everyone else.

She was back at the door and was knockin' and askin', could she come in? Raff motioned her in, and she said, Uncle Fury, oh, my, my Father had asked Carrie Jo to give this box to Miss Oatie.

We all gathered round to watch her open it. It was the prettiest little box, but was so small I didn't see how it could hold much! Oatie opened it and a fine piece of folded paper fell out. Oatie opened it and it said, "Here's the something new for my beloved new wife, and for our wonderful new life. I will love you always, Fury."

Well, you never saw such a flood of tears. Oatie had to sit down in her weddin' dress and all the wimmin was rushin' round tryin' to keep her dress from getting spotted. She hadn't even seen what the wrappin's was holdin' and you'd surely think she'd want to know what it was that was makin' her cry. I know we all sure did.

I sighed heavily and Martha patted my hand and said, "Be patient Lil, she'll get to it, it's just a very big day and very big happening. There, look she's opening the tissue – we'll soon know."

I said, "Well, she'll start cryin' again and it'll be time for supper and I haven't even tried my dress on." I knew my sour was comin' back and I was plenty ashamed of myself. Then I cheered right up cause now she had old and new. They were just two little rocks. She'd wear them stuck in her ears. They were called pearls and came from some kind of fish. Ugh! I wouldn't want no, *any* smelly fish rocks in my ears, but I guess they'd been cleaned up. So now with the borrowed and the blue, the good luck was sure to come back.

They were gettin' her out of her dress, and that meant I was next. Margaret Faye was sewin' the finishin' touches onto the weddin' dress, and out came my dress. It was wrapped in a sheet and when Raff took the sheet off, I gasped. It was my prettiest dress ever. My Mother's dress was a pale, pale purpley color, but mine was purple. It crinkled and made dear little sounds, and they all looked at each other's eyes and told me it was purple taffeta. It had flounces at the bottom and a sash in the back and it came to my ankles. It felt so good and I could twirl and it made such good swishin' sounds. I tried to stand real still so they could see if everything looked right.

I said, "Can you get the little mirror out so I can see us and see if my little Mam likes it and if she remembers me?"

Martha looked mixed up and Raff explained to her about me seein' my little Mam in the mirror and the dimple, and I so loved hearin' it again.

Oatie got a box from the corner where the weddin' finery had been and got me on a chair. She was takin' off my yellow shoes, and I was gettin' scared she'd think they wasn't fine enough for my dress and maybe I wouldn't get to be in the weddin'. I quick said, "Won't my yellow shoes look pretty with my dress? I just love yellow and purple."

Oatie said, ""Lil, I'm afraid your everyday shoes won't look very nice with this beautiful dress."

I thought my heart would break. I wasn't goin' to get to carry that little basket and throw them flowers and bows for Oatie, my Mother and Uncle Bear to walk on. Maybe I wouldn't even be allowed to watch, cause my beautiful yellow shoes wasn't fine enough. I could barely keep my tears back.

Martha was holdin' the box for them and they all said, "Now, squeeze your eyes shut, Lil, Martha has a surprise for you."

I squeezed 'em as hard as I could, mainly to keep those tears from fallin' on my dress and I was hearin' a rustlin' sound and the suckin' in of their breaths and they all said, "Open them, Lil!"

I opened 'em a little, then more, then I just opened 'em real big. There was a pair of black shiny, shiny shoes. They had a whole lot of straps and little teensy buttons to hold 'em. I didn't know what to think. I'd never seen nothin' like 'em. I looked at Martha. Her whole sweet face was beamin', so was everybody's. They was all covered with smiles. She said, "Lil, these are to be your dress-up shoes. You'll outgrow them, but we hope you and Clay will be the hit of this wedding in your finery. Darlin', those teensy little buttons are made of Mother-of-Pearl, so you and your Mother both have something new – pearls."

Oh no, my buttons are those smelly fish rocks. But I just loved the leather smell of my wonderful yellow shoes.

Martha continued, "These are one of the items little Runner happily made his trip back to Middleboro for. He felt so privileged to be able to bring your weddin' shoes. We had your footprint, which he took to Miss Marcy at the dry-goods store. He told us this was the most important errand he'd ever run."

Martha's eyes was twinklin' for sure, but I could tell there was tears tryin' to get out.

I couldn't help but sigh. I thought they were fine lookin' and I was proud to wear 'em, specially since poor little Runner had almost got dead tryin' to get 'em for me. I held 'em tight, up close to my face to see if they were stinky, and I couldn't smell 'em, so I smiled real big.

Martha said, "Oh Lil, I'm so happy you love 'em, and look what else!"

She held up some shiny socks. They were long and skinny and seemed to shimmer. I wondered if they was made out of stinky fish, too, but they were sort of pretty and didn't seem to smell either. The wimmin sat me down and pulled those socks on me and they went clear up to my knees. Then they put those black shiny shoes on my feet. They used a shoe spoon to make 'em go on easy. A shoe spoon! That was so funny to think of I had a gigglin' fit, but there they were on in the blink of an eye.

Martha laid that spoon down and picked up another funny looking thing. She said, "Lil, this is a button hook. You'll have to use it to button your dress-up shoes. You'll just love it because it's so much fun. See, you hold it like this (she put the handle in my hand) and stick the metal part through the slit in the strap. Then you grab the button like this and lean the buttonhook the other way. See, it slips that slit right over that button, and then you carefully remove the hook and go to the slit in the next strap! Isn't that fun? It will take you a while to get the knack of it, but once you do, you will be a real grownup lady! You'll see all the big girls and ladies will have hi-button shoes on for the wedding and you will, too! What do you think of that?"

My hand didn't seem to do it right and I was startin' to feel awful, but Martha reminded me about practicin' my violin or peelin' taters or fishin', or ridin' my horse. Nothin' is real good right off, but with some practicin', it all just gets fine. She said, "Lil, this set, the shoe spoon and the buttonhook, are my gift to you. Every lady must have one. You can keep them in your Miss Myrtle treasure box. Do you like that idea?"

I threw my arms around her neck and said, "Oh thank you, Martha, I just love 'em and now that I'll be five, I'll be a real lady and grownup, too."

She said, "Sweet child, I've been wishing most of my life for a little girl to spoil, and you've made me happier than I ever dreamed."

She held my hand with that buttonhook and in no time at all I had my first and best pair of hi-button shoes. It was such fun! When I got up to walk, I almost fell over they was so light on my feet, but they were my very best treasures. I looked so pretty from head to toe, and I couldn't wait to show my little Mam. My Mother was diggin' that mirror out, and I couldn't wait to see. I sure wisht I could see us from head to toe instead of the top part and the bottom part, but I would be able to see if my Mam was smilin' and her dimple was showin'.

We all got back in our regular clothes for the hoedown. I got to wear my blue checkered dress with the lace collar and pocket, and they put a new ruffled petticoat under it. I surely would like to wear my dress-up shoes, but I didn't want to get 'em dusty and dirty before the weddin'. My beautiful yellow shoes looked big and clunky somehow, but they felt friendly on my feet and I did love 'em. They tied a huge blue ribbon bow around some curls at the back of my head, and I felt so dressed up and so grownup. I bet Clay and Father, Uncle Bear, and Runner and best of all – Billy Joe – wouldn't even know who this new grownup girl was.

CHAPTER 6

What used to be our box house home had turned into a big town. I couldn't imagine that Middleboro could be any bigger. I wasn't quite so scared of it any more, but when I looked at our little box house, I got a big lump. It wasn't much bigger than the Wet Walker cabins. Raff and I both loved it and I think Martha did too. After tomorrow and the weddin', my Oatie Mother will be livin' in 2-house with my Father for a week and then us kids, me and Clay, will move in. I'm thinkin' they're not usin' their melons good, cause it would be such fun for the four of us to start our new livin' together at the same time.

I guess I been askin' a lot of questions. That's what Oatie, when she was still Oatie, used to teach me. She used to say to me, "Lil, if you don't ask questions, you'll never learn anything. Questions is always important and helps you get smarter. Be very sure to pay close attention to the answers cause they are even *more* important."

Well, looks to me like she has clean forgotten what she taught me, and it seems like all the big folks around me weren't taught that lesson at all. Lands, I had so many dumb answers that I'm beginnin' to wonder. Martha just changes the subject! I finally cornered Clay and asked him why on earth our Mother and Father had to stay by themselves and right next door?

He got all red in the face and stuttered and sputtered and said, "Lil, it's their honeymoon. When people get married, they go off together alone so's they can get to know each other better."

I guess I was starin' at him and was makin' him all antsy. His answer made about as much sense as anyone else's. I just sighed and thought to myself, I guess there's a mystery afoot. That leaves me two choices. I can ask Martha to tell me and if she starts talkin' about butterflies again, I'll just ask my Mother and Father! One minute I'm grow'd, grown up and have hi-button shoes, and the next minute I'm so little I can't get answers to my questions. I will be so glad when I get full grow'd and we're all the same age and can talk to each other! Whew – butterflies!!

It was lookin' like I might not get any more questions or answers this evenin'. The wimmin had put out tables full of sandwiches, sausages, greens, ham, and biscuits up at the tent town. Soon as they all filled up, they were gonna come down to that big empty ground where our meetin' house will be built this spring. They had boxes, empty from fixin' 2-house, big rolls of hay and slabs of wood balanced on empty nail kegs for the folks to sit on. They had caro-seen lanterns on poles to light it all up. They had a special place for the music folk to stand so's they wouldn't get bumped by all the dancin'. It wasn't dark yet, so them, those caro-seen lanterns wasn't lit. I could hardly wait. What a pretty place our home was, and I loved it filled with all these people. They just worked and worked and laughed and talked and sang. It was such a happy place with 'em all around us. I sure hope we wasn't lonely again when they left. Course, Martha would be stayin' and Runner and Pokey and little Ugly1 and Ugly2. I figured me and Dancer was gonna be takin' a lot of rides till they grow'd up!

The ladies and gents – that's short for gentlemen – had changed or at least cleaned up. Everyone I seen looked pretty spiffy. Oh I LOVED all my new words. One man had a squeeze-box. When I asked him about it, he pulled it apart and pushed it together and ran his fingers over some buttons, and 'bout knocked me flat. I never heard so much music noise come out of one little box. He said it was ah accordy-on. He wanted me to think it made better music than a violin, but I knew better. I just didn't say much cause I sure didn't want him to feel bad and go home. Oh, I hoped I could play Father's violin. I was tryin' to practice in my head like my Martha had told me, but it wasn't workin' yet. I so hoped I could make my Father and my Mother proud. I was thinkin' it could be my weddin' gift to them. I'll try to pray, no siree, I'll go find Raff and ask her to ask God-Willin' to help me play my songs right. Oh my, I sure am feelin' better. Lots of people have finished their supper and are comin' down.

I moseyed over to the cook fire to ask Martha if we were supposed to go eat. She told me to stay right there with her because Raff and the rest was goin' to bring food to us. That made me happy, cause Raff and I could pray while I was eatin'.

That fire was doin' a dance. The fiddlers were tunin' up, dusk was slippin' in, and I could feel the excitement. Two of the Preacher's and Margaret Faye's kids was startin' to light those lanterns, and I heard Father and Uncle Bear singin' and laughin', and here came our family. Uncle Bear was carryin' Runner, all wrapped in quilts, and they both was grinnin' from ear to ear. They made a seat of honor for him in the rockin' chair, close enough to the fire to stay warm, but so's he wouldn't miss a thing.

He called out, "Miss Lil, Miss Lil, I get to watch you and Clay dance. You two will have to do the dancin' for me this time, but next hoedown I'll be aleadin' 'em."

He looked so happy and so awful I didn't know which to pay attention to, so I just waved and waved at him and smiled and yelled, "I love you, Runner. After I eat, I'll come give you a hug."

Raff and Uncle Bear tucked him in and left him in Martha's caring hands. Raff and Uncle Bear came and Uncle Bear carried me to our box house porch. Raff spread out a little cloth, and I ate my fill but not before I asked her to pray for my violin playin'. She smiled at me and said, "Course I will, Lil."

Uncle Bear said, "Let's pray together, shall we?" He took Raff's hand and mine and bowed his head.

Raff looked at him a moment before she bowed hers, and I thought to myself I never seen her look so pretty. She had on a soft green dress with a white collar trimmed in lace. She had braided a green ribbon into her hair and it looked so beautiful.

No one could pray like my Raff Mam. She almost made prayers sound like singin'. I knew for sure God-Willin' would surely help me, so now I could relax and enjoy my first hoedown.

Clay came runnin' up and said, "Come on, Lil, let's go see Runner and then get a seat. I'll play some, but Martha and Father gave us permission to dance all we want to. You're to stay with Miss Martha and Runner or Margaret Faye if I'm playin'. Does that sound fine?"

I said, "That sounds fine, Clay. I supposed I'll be sittin' with Raff, but I guess she might dance, too. Oh Clay, I am so excited. I've never seen this many people. Do we know enough steps to dance? What if I forgot what you taught me?"

"Aw, Lil, don't worry. Just wait till you hear this music with all the fiddles, gee-tars and that accordy-on. You won't be able to sit still."

Raff and Uncle Bear listened to us. They chuckled and said, "Be off with you. We'll clean Lil's plate."

Raff said, "Clay, have you eaten anything yet?"

"I sure have, Raff, that's why I can't wait to dance. I'm full to poppin'."

They laughed again as we went runnin' over to Runner. Tears was runnin' down his cheeks but all he could say was, "I'm so happy, I love this family, and my new home. Me and Pokey and the new babes are so happy. I don't ever remember being this happy. I cain't thank none of you enough for this new life you gave me."

I didn't know whether to feel good or bad. It was too much for me, so I just looked for a spot that didn't look too broken or hurt and patted him and told him we loved him and was glad he was livin' the rest of his life with us. That God-Willin' would keep him safe and we'd keep him happy! I knew Oatie, I mean Mother and Raff would like that I told him that.

Clay was real nice, and they talked serious like, and then there come that idjit! Didn't they start talking about those rats agin? I started pullin' on him and tellin' Runner we'd be back. Clay looked confused, but I was determined to get near where all those fiddlers were tunin' up. My heart was poundin' with excitement like I'd never known. All those big kids were pairin' off and swingin' round to the tunin'. It was wonderful. Those lanterns was the prettiest things I'd ever seen and the cook fire was better than I ever seen it. Men and women, girls and boys was laughin' and talkin' and I was seein' a world I'd never seen. I was so happy I feared I'd start cryin'. If this was what a hoedown was like, then it would be my favorite treasure. I'd no sooner thought that than all those fiddlers, gee-tars and that music box started playin'. People was grabbin' their partners, they was yellin' and twirlin' and, oh, how can I say it 'cept, if this was sent from God-Willin', I surely wanted to always be his child. Oh the joy! It was somethin' I'd never seen. It was so happy and everyone was havin' so much fun I could hardly stand it. The ground was covered with the young people and people like my Father and Mother. Clay and I just stopped and watched. We could hardly get our breath. We was both watchin' our new Mother and Father and they were the best. They were wondrous.

We saw Martha talkin' to Raff and Uncle Bear and swooshin' them off to the dance floor. She was twinklin', laffin', and clappin' her hands. She came over to us and took each of us by the hands. She said, "I hope you children will always remember this. I know Lil will, because it's her first. But, Clay, this is God's gift to us. Our friendship and all that has come from people giving all they have to benefit others. This is charity. This is love. This is the real meaning to our life. Isn't it beautiful?"

I was so star struck I couldn't talk. I couldn't take my eyes off my Mother and Father. My Mother was so beautiful she brought tears to my eyes. My Father was so handsome I didn't know what to think. They never took their eyes off each other. I wanted to grow up and be like them. I asked Martha, "Martha, why do my Mother and Father look at each other the way they do. Why do they look like that, what does it mean?"

Martha said, "Lil, that's love. That's what love looks like when two people fall in love. Darlin' girl, don't ever forget this. When you grow up, you need someone to look at you just the way Fury is lookin' at Oatie. Remember that, Lil. Remember that – forever."

I looked at Martha. Her eyes was all starry and she looked happier in a way I never seen. I could see shiny tears but they was all happy. I had that shiver go through me and now that I knew what it was, I promised my Martha I would always remember that wondrous time of my life. All of a sudden, I saw where she was lookin'. Oatie and Fury were at one end and they were mashed together like a sandwich, but Martha was lookin' towards the other end of the dance floor, and there was Uncle Bear and Raff. They was lookin' at each – well, they was lookin' at each other pretty much the way my Father and Mother was alookin'. I was mixed up, but she looked so happy.

Clay, the idjit, was stompin' and clappin' and sayin', "C'mon, Lil, let's go dance."

But I was like I was frozen in one spot. Martha looked happier than I've ever seen her. She had the sweetest smile on her face. I didn't know what to do, so I said, "Martha, is everything all right, are you happy?"

She turned, looked in my eyes and said, "Lil, I can't tell you how happy I am. You see, Lil. All's well that ends well. I am finally at peace." She leaned down and kissed me and said, "Now, go try out your steps with Clay. They'll be playin' a slow waltz and then the quadrille. I can't wait to watch you. Runner and I will be cheerin' you on."

Clay and I did so good and I was proud. We did our little waltz pretty good, and I loved the quadrille. All the big kids acted like I was just like them. I danced a waltz with Unc-Father and Uncle Bear, but I danced hoedown music with Billy Joe. It was the best time of my life. Then Father and I played our songs.

Father carried me into the house. I could still hear the music, but as he said, I was out on my feet. My Mother dressed me for bed. Uncle

Bear carried Runner back to the tent, and Martha and Raff sat by the fire with their heads together, holdin' hands and talkin'. Mother and Father went for a little walk. Miss Myrtle said she was afraid I'd never come to bed, and with all the happy thoughts dancin' in my head and the memory of everyone clappin' after God-Willin' helped me play the violin. I thought how glad I was that God-Willin' was takin' care of me and my family that I loved so.

It was then I remembered Martha's happy words to me. "It's all's well that ends well, I am finally at peace." I wanted to keep those words – always.

CHAPTER 7

Everyone should open their eyes in the morn and hear sweet singin'. It's like knowin' all those angels with their wings is gonna carry you through the day. It's the happiest feeling in this whole world. I guess it makes every day the happiest day ever. Seems like since I've started livin', my days has been filled with so many wonders and treasures. My little Mam and Pap sure loved me a lot to leave me where my Oatie and Raff Mams could find me and take me for their own and give me this fine world. Seems like I'm so filled with love for all the goodness around me that it's hard to think I've had sour days. I'm so ashamed! I don't even 'member sayin' my prayers last night, but I must've, cause this day has to be a special gift.

I can hear busy going on, but it's not like the excitement of the hoedown. I'll never, ever forget that night. It was so filled with noise and color and … excitement. Everyone was excited, excited and so-o-o happy. I heard more music than I knew there was. The fiddlers and gee-tars and that box just made you want to jump and holler. When Uncle Fury, Father played our sweet song, there wasn't a sound from all those people and then when he tucked his violin under my chin and I played my three songs, I thought maybe everyone had gone away. I'm happier closing my eyes when I play – like my Martha told me – so I didn't know if the folks was still there till I finished.

The people yelled and clapped and Father took my hand, winked his eye at me and said, "Give 'em your famous curtsy, Lil."

It was like people couldn't get enough. They wanted me to play again, but Father swooped me and the violin up in his arms, grabbed Oatie's hand – the one that wasn't wiping away tears, of course, and they carried me off to bed. They both told me how well I did and how proud they was, *were*. They said everbody was crying. I felt all swelled up and couldn't wait to go to sleep on account of the happy dreams I knew was waitin' for me.

This mornin', it seems like last night was all a dream. I heard a noise and saw somethin' move, and my Oatie Mam, my beautiful Mother got up and came and sat beside me. She wrapped her arms around me and made me so glad I was her child. She said, "Lil, Lil, what a wonder and a treasure you are. How are we so lucky?"

She made me feel so happy when she was talkin' special just to me, in her quiet way. I hugged her and tried to tell her how much I loved her and my life and how I never knew I was a treasure. I said, "Why are you sittin' all quiet in here? Are you all right? Is it still your weddin' day? Shall I get up and get ready to help everyone?"

"Lil, I've been sitting here enjoying the peace and quiet and holding my Mother's little Bible. I mean to give it to the Preacher to read out of."

I said, "Kin I see it and touch it and hold it before you give it away? It was my very own Grandmother's, you see. It'll be like I'm touchin' her. Please, please."

Oatie looked at me and smiled that sweet beautiful smile I loved and said, "Lil, darlin', this little Bible will be yours. Raff and I have already talked it over and decided after the wedding today, the Bible will be yours. That way you will grow up with it and use it for your wedding and then give it to your own little girl."

I knew my eyes was big. I said, "How old will I be when I get married and have a little girl?"

Oatie laughed and said, "Oh Lil, it won't be till you're grown up. We just wanted it to be yours now."

"Whew," I said, "I'm sure glad cause Martha told me last night that when I grow up and fall in love I would want someone to look at me the way Unc-Father was looking at you. She said that was love and it was supposed to be like that. Like Uncle Bear was lookin' at Raff. But since I don't rightly know of anyone who looks at me like that, I was 'bout to start worryin'."

Oatie was starin' at me.

I said, "What's wrong? Should I be gettin' my bath water? Should I put on my overalls till we climb in our wedding finery? Are you scared, Oatie? Is it cause you think you don't know Uncle Fury? Oh Oatie-Mother what's wrong? Why are you starin' at me?"

She asked me about everythin' Martha said, and I told her, and it all seemed good. It was mostly about my Mother, but Martha said the prettiest, sweetest words when she was watchin' Raff and Uncle Bear. I was hopin' that my Mother was worried for fear everyone was seein' how she and Father loved each other and she'd start that turnin' red thing again. I said how glad I was that our families loved each other so much.

Oatie shook her head and put her head in her hands, then straightened up and said, "Let's pop you into a wonderful warm bath and then into a pair of clean overalls. I'm sure you can stay clean and sweet till four PM." She laughed and I was sure glad. These weddin's sure do strange things to people. Maybe I'm not sure I want to do a weddin', but I guess I won't get me a little girl if don't do a weddin'. My heart was heavy.

Oatie lifted my chin, looked into my eyes and said, "Lil, what was that sigh for?"

I looked at her and said, "I was just thinkin' about how hard it seems to be to get me a little girl. I'm sure glad I've got some time!"

She hugged me good and said, "Get your clothes laid out, Lil, and I'll go get a tub of warm water. Raff's cookin' at the cook fire and Martha and the wimmin are dressin' up the altar – that's where the Preacher will stand. After we get you sparklin', I'll help you fluff the bed and tidy up your room. How does that sound? Remember, we'll be getting dressed in here!"

I nodded as hard as I could and she went out the door. I got to thinkin', I was so-o-o hungry, maybe she could bring me a biscuit and a little slab of bacon. I went to the door to call to her and I saw her and Raff holdin' each other, and it looked like they was both bawlin'. Then my pretty sweet smellin' Martha slowly made her way to the cook fire. She pulled them apart and looked from one to another as she was talkin'. Oh, I wisht I could hear what those three wimmin was sayin'. All of a sudden, Martha had her arms around each of them and was lookin' towards God-Willin' and sayin', "Thanks be to God."

They all just kept huggin' and cryin'. My Martha looked up and saw me in the door and waved and blew me a kiss. Oatie-Mother grabbed the tub of water and started up to the box house. Raff quick grabbed the other side and Martha called after them, "I'll fix her a plate and bring it up there. I may make us all a cup of tea and we'll have us a grand bathin' party."

They all was either laughin' or cryin', I couldn't tell which, but we were goin' to be together, and that was good.

Last night was so filled with color and excitement and this day was gentle and calm and everthin' was peaceful. I told 'em all and they said I was a very smart child. I liked that a lot. They said a great, great big word that I was, and my eyes must have told them it was way too big, so they changed it to smart. That suited me better. We wimmin drank our tea while I munched on my bacon and my biscuit slathered with elderberry jam. They was chattin' and laughin' and Martha was tellin' stories, and we were all havin' fun. I didn't understand very much, but I laughed with 'em so they'd think I did, and I didn't even care if they knew. I just loved 'em all.

After I dressed, we went and looked at the altar and it was covered with trailin' ivy. The big boys had gone into the woods and dug up big ferns. They had cut nail kegs in half and planted them and placed them around everywhere. They were beautiful.

My Oatie-Mother kept puttin' her hands over her mouth she was so thrilled. There was lots more of them than the fingers on both my hands and they had ribbons around them. Seems Runner had brought bolts of ribbon from the dry-goods lady so you could never believe this pretty, quiet spot was filled with music and dancin' just last night.

They'd made benches for people to sit on and I was thrilled. They'd made an aisle for all of us to walk down. I really felt like a princess. Margaret Faye's sister made weddin' cakes. She and her husband come up here in a buggy at noon yesterday. They were stayin' for the hoedown, weddin' and would be the first guests in one of the Wet Walker cabins. Margaret Faye told Martha that her sister made all the parts and trims, and would stack it together up here and frost it. Margaret Faye said, "Have you ever?" all the time, and I guess I had been sayin' it a lot. I thought it sounded big and important, especially when I didn't understand somethin', but I'm thinkin' I didn't fool many of the folks.

When they told me about stackin' that cake, I wanted to say somethin' grow'd, grown up, I said, "Have you ever?"

That got Martha to laughin' so hard she almost fell off the bench she was tryin' out. They all laughed and even though they hugged me and said they was laughin' "with me" – they wasn't, cause I wasn't laughin'!

Martha patted the bench beside her and said, "Come over here, darlin', so's we can all have a little discussion. Seems like a "sour spell" might be comin' on and land sake, we certainly don't want that on the day of the weddin', do we?"

I moped over and plunked down beside her. I smelled her good smell and felt a little better but not much.

Martha put her arms around me and said, "Lil, Lil, it's hard growin' up. Especially for a bright little star like you. You want to be grown up and we all love and adore you just as you are. What shall we do about this? You do need to realize that you have a very natural knack for being funny. Lucky you. Makin' people laugh is the best medicine in the whole world. Almost everyone I know would love to be able to make others laugh. Lil, it's one of God's greatest gifts. My sweet child, He has blessed you with so many that we are constantly surprised. You must start being grateful and start being happy about all these grand talents – I know we sure are."

She raised my mopey chin up so we was lookin' in each other's eyes and hers was a-dancin', and she was smilin' so big at me I just had to grin. This was the best day for my Mother and Father and I was actin' like sour milk. Whew, this is gonna be a mighty hard road to be a grownup if I keep makin' it so bumpy. I told 'em all right then, I was not gonna be sour no more, and I'm glad I made 'em laugh cause I liked us all to be happy. I told 'em when I got my little girl she more'n likely wouldn't want her mother to be full of sour milk!

Clay came runnin' up to see what we were doin' and decided to walk with us. He'd been up since dawn and he said it had been wonderful. Nobody wanted to go home to Middleboro cause they loved bein' up here so much. He said they were all sorry it was this far done and they couldn't wait till spring so they could come back. Since he was my brother and my first friend, I thought I should tell him the news, so I said, "Clay, I'm growin' up and I'm through with the sour milk." I was proud and I thought he'd be so happy, but he was lookin' at me like he'd never seen me before! What's wrong with him? Martha got to laughin' again and had to sit down on a big rock. They explained to him and he giggled too. I was just about to think sour and then I started laughin' too.

He scratched his head and said, "I don't know if I'll ever figure you out, Lil, but you're my sister and first friend and I surely do love you anyway."

I said, "Clay that will do just fine, I love you too."

We walked clear around the complex and talked to all the workers. They seemed thrilled about the weddin' and was talkin' and singin' softly. They all seemed happy and excited and almost sad that our barn-raisin' was about over. They said they were tying up loose ends. I'm thinkin' that's a sayin', but I'll have to listen more to get it straight.

Most of the women were in 2-house dressin' it up for the honeymoon. There were lots of things I didn't know, but I figgered my melon was plenty full and I just needed to be happy about that. I was tryin' to do a lot of listenin' so's I could ask questions later. That seemed like the smart thing to do and I sure wanted to keep bein' smart.

I was wonderin' why we hadn't seen Father and Uncle Bear and Billy Joe. Clay said they were all in the tent with Runner. Then he said, "Lil, wait till you see those pups. They are gettin' so sweet I'm gettin' as sad as you are cause we can't pick 'em up and love 'em."

I 'membered to just listen, instead of sayin' anything to him when he was bein' an idjit! Ugh, I forgot we'd have to look at the rats. He said, "Oatie-Mother, you and Uncle Fury can't see each other before the weddin', so you can't see these darlin' pups."

Martha and Raff said, "Land sake, Oatie, we almost forgot about that, you better go back to our box house cook fire and stir up a little light lunch, and we'll see the men and the pups, and then we'll come back and join you."

My Oatie-Mother laughed and looked so happy that I just knew she must have seen Ugly1 and Ugly2 and was glad she didn't have to do that again. I didn't know why she and Uncle Fury couldn't see each other, but I'd whisper a question about it to Martha. Oatie-Mother left our group to head for the box house and we headed on to that dreadful tent. Suddenly, I 'membered that dear little Pokey was in there, and so was Runner, so I cheered right up. We could hear the men talkin' and laughin' easy like, and I felt happy and warm inside, and I for sure was gonna let Pokey see I was doin' better and comin' to see her pups.

Clay ran ahead and hollered at the men and they pulled the flap back and ushered us in. Runner was lookin' better and told me he cried when I played the violin last night. I looked up at my Father and smiled, and he held his arms out and I was in 'em. When he held me, nothin' was wrong with my world. I loved him so. Uncle Bear and

Billy Joe was goin' on about how well I did, and Father whispered in my ear, "Would you like to give these fine friends who love you a big thank you?" We looked at our eyes and I put my fingers on his nose and kissed it.

I said, "Thank you kindly."

I could tell everyone thought that was pretty grown up and I was glad, but Father was walkin' me towards that dreaded box. I looked down and saw that precious little Pokey lookin' at me. Her tail was waggin' so fast like it was tellin' me how glad she was to see me. Father put me down and I put my hand on her soft, soft head and stroked her like I did Dancer. She closed her eyes like she loved it, and I made my eyes look at the Ugs. They had grown hair. Not a lot, but they didn't look like rats so much. They were makin' little squeaky sounds and they were almost cute. Pokey's tail was waggin' so hard it kept brushin' against one of 'em and when it did, the little thing would make a tiny squeal. We was all laughin' at it and I was beginnin' to think maybe this was all gonna work out fine.

Uncle Bear had his arm around Martha and kissed the top of her head. He said, "Since Fury can't see Oatie till the weddin', we're going to send him up here to have lunch and we'll be joining you ladies – if that's all right?"

Raff said, "I can hardly believe time is goin' so fast. It's almost noon. Everything seems well on its way to being finished. After lunch, we'll go into the little box house, finish the bride's bouquet and a few other items and then leisurely prepare ourselves for this great day. I have to admit I'm thrilled and excited."

Uncle Bear took Raff's hand and kissed her on the forehead. Billy Joe picked me up and kissed my dimple and said, "How's my Lady Fair? Are you ready for your first wedding? Somehow I feel you may enjoy it every bit as much as the bride and groom. Oh, and by the way, after learnin' how beautifully you dance, Miss Lil, I'd like to request the first dance with you at your folks' reception. What do you think?"

What I thought was, how glad I was he was holdin' me cause if he wasn't, I knew I'd be fallin' in a heap!

Uncle Bear said, "We'll be comin' back up here to get Runner all dressed up for the weddin' and of course we'll try to make your Pa presentable. I don't know what we'll do with Billy Joe, but we'll do our best." I knew they was all just havin' fun because it was a happy, happy day.

Clay and I finished our lunch and was talkin' about the weddin' and reception and dancin'. Oatie Mother and Martha were tendin' to last minute things and Raff was washin' the dishes and Uncle Bear was dryin' them.

I said, "Clay do you think Uncle Bear and Raff love each other?"

Clay didn't even stop to think, he said, "Why, course they do, why wouldn't they?"

I said, "Well, because he has Martha and he loves her too."

Clay just looked at me. Then he said, "Lil, do you love Uncle Fury?" I nodded and he said, "Do you love Uncle Bear?" I nodded and he said, "Well, do you love me?" I nodded and he said, "Well, do you love Billy Joe?" I nodded and he said, "Well, do you love Runner and Pokey and the pups?"

I kind of nodded, cause those pups was still not winnin' my heart, then I 'membered my silent promise to Pokey and nodded real good.

He said, "See there, Lil, you love all these people. That should show you, there's lots of room for love. I'm thinking a nice thing for you to do would be to let your melon have a nice rest till after the weddin'. How does that sound?"

He was grinnin' so big I got tickled. No wonder everyone was so sick of my questions. My melon was an idjit. We was soon laughin' out loud, and I vowed to him I'd give my melon a good nap till after the weddin'.

Martha helped me button my hi-button shoes. Soon as we finish, I'll be ready, and the first one, too. I wisht they wasn't all so busy and flutterin' cause I'd sure love to look in that mirror to see my little Mam and me again. That mirror was plenty busy and was goin' from one to another, though, so I'll just have to wait. They made a weddin' bouquet for my Mother and it was so pretty. It was filled with those ro-do-drens, the whole flower, and had ivy and ferns all around it. It was tied with purple, lavender and white trailin' ribbons, and we all thought Martha was wonderful cause she could do so many things.

That red-headed Carrie Jo was in the box house helpin' us all get ready. She'd go out and peek ever' so often and she said some people were already sittin' in their seats and seemed to be just relaxin'. She said everyone she could see sure was dressed up and looked mighty fine.

I wish I hadn't put my melon to sleep 'cause I couldn't seem to think of words big enough to say how Oatie-Mother – I've got to think Oatie, but say Mother, else I'm about to become annoying. Martha says that's almost a sin! Anyways, how Mother looks. She's so pretty all the time and I've seen her when she's just beautiful, but I've never seen her look like this. She and Raff got their hair washed and almost brushed dry and then they tied it in rags. I thought I'd faint at the looks and if I was Unc-F-Father, I'd surely run away real fast. They took those things off a while ago and I swear I never saw anythin' that looked that pretty. Their hair had soft waves and shined and gleamed and made me wish I had that kind of hair. Course I sure wouldn't want to wear those rags. Well, Martha and Raff just put a circle of silk on the top of Mother's head and a beautiful piece of lace hung down her back. She picked up her bouquet and ever'one just gasped. She looked like a beautiful queen. Raff leaned over and kissed her on both cheeks, and they just stood and looked at each other.

Mother said, "Raff, can this be true? Is this real, or should I pinch myself to be sure?"

Raff laughed and said, "Martha, what do you think, is all this really happening?"

Martha gave her tinklin' laugh that I loved and said, "Looking at Oatie and you, Raff, I feel like I'm in the presence of royalty. I've never seen such beautiful women, and add Miss Lil to that mix and it's truly overwhelming."

Everyone's cheeks was such a pretty pink and I'm sure hopin' mine are too. I don't know where that mirror went, so I guess I'll just have to hope.

Carrie Jo came back in and she was flushed. She leaned against the door and Raff said, "Carrie Jo, something tells me you just caught a glimpse of that young handsome lad you're sweet on."

She turned bright red and grinned a big grin and said, "I sure did, and he's holding a seat for me. My Father said as soon as the music starts, you're all to go out and stand by him. Martha first, then Raff, then Clay who, by the way, is already there and looks very handsome, then Lil, and then – the bride. Daddy says he's placing Fury behind the tree in the garden so he won't catch sight of Oatie till she starts down the aisle. Oh, I'm gonna cry, I just know it, and my nose gets all red and I don't even have a hanky and I don't know where my Mother is to get one. I'm so excited I could faint."

I perked up at that. The nose gettin' all red didn't do much for me, but I sure was hopin' she'd faint. It would be my first sightin' of a faintin' lady. Ever'one was so busy calmin' her down and gettin' her a hanky that I guess they didn't realize that seein' someone faint was kind of important to me. She was lookin' better, so I guess I wasn't goin' to see it today. I was a little disappointed, but I wouldn't let anyone know it.

Then I heard it, oh my, oh my. Is there anythin' in the world more beautiful than violin music? My heart felt as tho it might stop. Ever'one's eyes was glistenin' with tears and smilin' at the same time. Oh, how I wanted a weddin'. This was the best, the very best.

Martha went out, then Raff stopped, gave me a kiss and said, "Here's our happy wedding day, Lil. We love you. Follow me, darlin'."

I looked back at my beautiful Mother and she came to me, knelt down, kissed my dimple, and said, "Your Father and I will love you forever, Lil, know that, my sweet child, and walk with us into our new world."

My happy tears was streamin' and so were hers and neither of us cared.

I was so proud followin' Clay and sprinklin' my flowers and bows. I could see Father staring behind me, and I didn't even have to look, cause I had their look of love for each other etched into my heart. I stood in my place at the altar and watched Uncle Bear hand my Mother over to my Father. Clay got closer to me and took my hand. I was glad.

Then it was over. They was kissin' like they was stuck.

I was gonna say somethin', but Clay squeezed me real hard and said, "Li-i-i-l-l, remember what I told you." I didn't even get a chance to nod cause Father swooped me up in his arms and Mother grabbed Clay, and our family walked back down the aisle. Ever'one was standin' and clappin' and cheerin' and cryin', and I guess I'd never seen anythin' this fine and happy.

I looked over Father's shoulder at Raff and Billy Joe. They stopped for Martha, and she grabbed Billy Joe's elbow, and Raff and Uncle Bear followed 'em. Then the Preacher and Margaret Faye slowly helped little Runner. Everyone was full of smiles and I thought to myself …

Good, better, best.

CHAPTER 8

A *reception* is where you welcome all your friends to your new life. It's when you *receive* them and make them glad they're your friends. You serve them good food and somethin' to drink (they was havin' a milk punch, which I wasn't allowed to go near, neither was Clay), and a fruit punch for all the young'uns and people who didn't prefer spirits. I'd woke up my melon and pestered my Martha until she told me three whole times so I'd be sure to know it. Clay told me to put my melon back to bed before I became annoyin'. Since that was a sin, I vowed to let it miss the *reception* cause my road was bumpy enough without addin' sins.

The boys was playin' music while people lined up to kiss the bride and shake Father's hand. I sure was glad they feared we'd get antsy standin' in that line, so we were allowed to walk around and look at ever'body's weddin' finery and watch 'em all an' listen. Preacher Jackson and Margaret Faye had seven kids of their own. They were all red haired an' freckled and sweet as pie. Four boys an' three girls. Martha told us everyone was nicer than the next one. I was ready to work on that sayin', but Clay said, "Li-i-i-l, leave it be."

I was just afraid I'd forget somethin', but since he reminded me I'd vowed, I just let it be.

The evenin' was cool and ever'body had a shawl around their shoulders. The lacy shadows was all there as the sun went down, but it was all soft and creamy. It was easy and peaceful. I was tryin' to describe it to Clay, so he'd know what I was feelin', but I couldn't seem to find the words that matched my seein'.

He said, as he stopped in the path, "Lil, just close your eyes and think of what it makes you feel like. Think of something that you love or that tastes good or feels good, maybe even smells good."

I squeezed my eyes shut and sniffed and thought and thought and thought. I was about to give up on it when all of a sudden I knew. I said, "Close your eyes real tight, Clay, while I tell you." He did, and I said, "Remember when we get up early on a Saturday morn and go for a little walk before breakfast or to feed the animals? When we come back, it feels like everthin' is lazy and easy. Oatie or Raff pulls out a big pan of white fluffy biscuits with their tops all golden like. You carefully slide one on your plate, and it opens up and wisps of steam puff out of it and you put a hunk of fresh butter on it and it melts away till you're wonderin', was it ever there? They pour you a mug of creamy white cold, cold milk and you sit down in the green, good smellin' grass and you eat it. That's what this whole reception is like to me. Open your eyes, Clay, do you see what I mean, can you feel it? Can you see it and smell it?

He finally said, "Never in all my ten years would I think of this beautiful, peaceful reception as being like eatin' a biscuit for breakfast."

I said, "Clay, it's like it's white and creamy. The coverin's for the tables is white. The ribbons around the ferns are white, that weddin' cake that's taller'n me is all white with white roses coverin' it. The petals and ribbons in my little basket are white. The flowers Mother carried are white, your pillow was white. Don't you see?"

He thought a minute and finally said, "Lil, I give up. I don't think your melon's been asleep for a minute. I swan if I don't almost see what you're seein'. I guess I thought last night was so pretty – with all the colors and excitement."

I said quietly, "Well, Clay, I think there's different shades of pretty."

I was just a little kid and I didn't have words. Seems like I missed my whole start, so it's hard sometimes to catch up. I felt disappointed in me, that I couldn't tell Clay how beautiful our home looked and felt. How I loved ever'body and everthin' and how happy I was. Everthin' mattered to me, and biscuits was about my favorite treat.

People were moseyin' around, lots of 'em was holdin' hands and laughin' and talkin'. It was important to me cause they all said, "hey Lil" and "hey Clay." It was so much fun cause they all knew our names. We said "hey" back and I felt like I knew a whole town full of people. They were admirin' all that they'd help build and we were like a great big family. We walked back to the reception and stood in front of that big cake. The sun was slowly sinkin', but I think it was takin' its time cause it was still a glowin'. As I looked up at that beauty of a cake, I saw that the top of it was completely covered with that pretty golden glow I was tryin' to tell Clay about.

I looked up at him quick and he looked down at me, grinned, and said, "All right, all right, Lil, I see it."

It made me so glad, I had to jump up and down and clap. We found a log and sat on it so's we could watch the goin's on and wait for the kissin' and hand shakin' to finish. I was plenty happy cause Clay knew what I meant. He had hold of my hand, and I squeezed it and I looked up at him. There was big ol' fat tears drippin' out of his eyes.

I said, "Clay, what's wrong? Why are you so sad?"

It was like he dumped a big bucket of water. He was sobbin', but he said, "I'm really happy, Lil, it's just that I'll never, ever see my sweet Father again. He was such a great Dad, Lil, in every way. I don't think about it much because of Uncle Fury and how, well, how he's become my, our Father, but ever so often I miss my Dad so much and I see his sweet handsome face and – the memories – oh Lil, I'm so sorry. I'm sorry for blubberin' like this, it's just, just that all of this is everything it should be, and then my Father's face is there and I'm so sad for a bit."

I didn't have nothin' to help him wipe his eyes, but he just took both of his hands and mopped at the tears. I said, "Clay, I don't feel very good sayin' this when you're hurtin' so much but, well … I had a sad time this mornin' 'cause I can't hardly member what my little Pap looked like. I know he was sad and scared, hungry and cold, but I can't see his face at all. Truth is Clay, he scared me a little. His eyes were scary but they was soft and gentle when he looked at my little Mam, but other times they looked fierce and wild. His hair was long and straggly, and I just can't get his face no more. I feel so sad, but it's hard to cry over him, and yet I know I should. See Clay, I can see my little Mam in the mirror, so I'll be able to see her forever … but he's gone, he's just … gone from me."

By now, we was both bawlin'. The shakin' and kissin' was over and that bunch of people was headin' for the cake. Mother and Father saw us two pitiful soppy children sittin' there and, land sakes, what did they think? They came runnin' over to us and gathered us, and Father took his hanky and cleaned us up. We was both talkin' at once, but they knew immediately. Dear beautiful Mother wrapped her arms around Clay and rocked him and shushed him and Unc-Father had me in his arms shushin' me and rockin' me. I guess they was through with their weddin' clothes, because they were fast on the way to gettin' messed up pretty bad. I was nuzzled into my good place and my tears and hiccups was stoppin', and I heard Clay laugh a little.

Father said, "What do you say to you two helpin' us to cut this big beautiful cake? We'll give you two the very first pieces with roses and frosting galore. You can both sit there while we see that all these fine hungry people finish their eatin' with a piece of this unbelievable cake. Then we will all start the dancin'. How does that sound to you?"

I looked at Clay's eyes and we both managed a watery smile and said how much we'd like that.

The four of us cut some of the cake, and Clay and I happily sat on our log and let visions of our lost Paps return to their heavens.

When the folks had finished, there wasn't nearly the cake left that I thought there'd be, but I didn't care cause I was stuffed. So was Clay.

I said, "Clay does your heart feel better?"

He patted my hand and said, "Yes it does, Lil, you're such a good sister. I can't tell you all the sadness I feel at times, but you're my sadness chaser. I'd only ever been around grownups, and to have a friend like you has made it easier to deal with all my scares and worries. I love you Lil, and I surely do thank God-Willin' for you ... Lil, your face is pink, are you blushin'?"

I quick felt my cheeks and sure enough they was warm. I didn't know if I'd done that before, but Clay sayin' lands sakes all those sweet things to me made me feel squirmy. I think because I knew how many sour awful things I'd done. Seems like there's two of me. He was talkin' so nice to the nice Lil, but I knew that other willful, naughty, sour Lil was hidin' behind a tree.

—ᴍ—

The fiddlers and the music folk were gettin' ready for the dancin'. The first dance would be our Mother and Father, then the weddin' party was to dance. Martha and Uncle Bear, Raff and Billy Joe, and me and Clay. Then they was goin' to have a quadrille – my very favorite. Billy Joe had already said he was claimin' me for the dance.

Clay had asked the youngest Jackson girl to dance with him. She's almost thirteen and is way taller than Clay. He said, "Lil, I'm a little nervous cause she's so much taller than me."

I said, "Don't be a dunce, Clay. She doesn't care, 'sides you're the finest lookin' boy here, next to Billy Joe that is. Look how tall Billy Joe is. Lands, Clay, we're goin' to have a wonderful time. Oh, oh, our dance is about over. Looks like Father and Mother are going to sit this one out and watch. Aren't you proud Clay? Now don't make a silly mistake! E-E-E-E-E-E-E!

"Gotcha," Billy Joe said as he swept me up to his shoulder.

I was gigglin' so hard I could hardly talk, but I stuck my feet out and said, "Lookit, Billy Joe, look at my hi-button shoes!"

"I love 'em, Lil, they're just beautiful. Hope they don't ruin your dancin'."

I squeaked out "They won't," as he stood me up across from him.

Oh my, it was so fine I could have kept dancin' till I just fell in a heap. At the end of it, Billy Joe bowed like a gentlemen and I did the prettiest curtsy I'd ever done. I knew my cheeks was pink cause they were warm under my hands.

Billy Joe said, "Lil, you're the best. I wish you were eighteen years old. I can't believe you can dance like a grown up."

I twirled around I was so happy, When I did I caught a glimpse of Uncle Fury, my Father. He and Oatie were both starin' at me with wide awful-lookin' eyes. Father was like he was a frozen stick and my Mother was sobbin'. I grabbed Billy Joe and looked up at him. He saw where I was lookin' and swept me up in his arms and walked us over to the two of them. People were clappin' and yellin' for me to do another curtsy. I was so scared, I clung to Billy Joe's neck.

He reached his other hand out and grabbed my Father and said, "Fury, Fury what is it, what's happening?"

About that time I felt strong arms take me out of Billy Joe's arms and hand me to Raff. Uncle Bear said, "Raff, dear, take Lil to Martha, please."

Raff carried me over to Martha and we three sat down. Raff got up and went to the boys with the violins and told them to keep playin', and to make it lively. When she came back and told us what she'd told them, Martha finally smiled. I was scared to death. What had happened? What's wrong with our Father and Mother?

I asked Raff, and she said, "Lil, I don't rightly know, but I have the feeling it's going to be all right." She looked at Martha and said, "He looked like he'd seen a ghost."

Martha said, "Raff, I thought the same thing."

We sat and watched the dancers. They were havin' a wonderful time and didn't seem to know there'd been a happenin'.

The cluster of men around Uncle Fury and Oatie was talkin' and kinda millin' around.

Martha said, "Raff, I think you need to go and see if Oatie needs you. Lil and I will be fine. Besides, that way you can find out what's going on!" She and Raff smiled a little.

Raff said, "That's very true, my dear, I'll ignore our best known fact that you are Nosy Nellie."

Martha smiled and said, "Maybe I'm nosy because I'd rather know the truth than let my very active imagination loose."

Raff said, "You're right, love, I'll be back as quickly as I can."

Martha stretched her shawl so that it went around her and me. I wanted to know my Father and Mother were all right. I was shiverin'.

Clay came over to where we were sittin' and said, "Uncle Bear told me to come get Lil and get out there and dance, that everything will be fine, and it will make them feel better real fast if they see we're okay. I sure don't feel like it, but, Lil, I'm thinkin' we better dance."

I looked at Martha and her eyebrows was raised up and she said, "Well, yes sireebob, if Uncle Bear says you're to dance, I surely do think I'd do just that. What do you think, Lil?"

I looked back at Clay and he kinda looked like he'd lost his best friend or like somebody had kicked him in the seat of his trousers. Like Clay, I surely didn't want to get on the wrong side of Uncle Bear, so I said, "Well Clay, I don't know of no, *any* more weddin's comin' up, so if we want to dance, I guess we need to get up and out on the dance floor." He nodded and held out his hand. I kissed Martha and off we went. I loved to dance and so did Clay. He was a good dancer and a good teacher. His sweet Father had taught him and he said he'd been a strict teacher. Clay taught me how to waltz and do a Schottische and a point toe and a two-step and quadrilles and a dosey doe thing and we had the most fun. It was fun doin' it without music, but it was so much more fun with real music. I kept trying to catch a glimpse of our Mother and Father.

Clay yelped. He said, "Listen here Miss Nosy Britches, you just stepped on my foot. You better pay attention or I'll take you back to Martha and go get Millie Jackson." He was pretendin' to frown but my eyes must have gotten big, cause he said, "Aw-w-w-w-w, Lil, I'm just funnin' with you. She's a good dancer but not near as good as you, course since I taught you how to dance it's no wonder you're good!" We both laughed and he bowed and I did another curtsy, and a bunch of the big kids clapped, and one of the girls asked me to teach her how to curtsy that pretty. I was so thrilled I knew my cheeks were red.

Raff went back finally and sat with Martha. Martha just looked at her friend and knew Raff would say her piece when she was ready. "Well Martha," Raff said, "I'm certainly glad you're gonna be my roommate. There's so much you don't know about our little Princess. A lot of it will break your heart, my sweet friend, but the majority will have you singing her praises. Martha, when Fury was at the wedding of his brother (Clay's Father) he actually witnessed Lil's little Mother (who was twelve at the time) dancing with her father. After you read the letter her father left …" Martha's eyes grew huge – yes, we have – "I guess you'd call it his last will and testament. It's heart breaking, but thank God we have it. It explains so much. The whole thing has affected Fury profoundly. You know the worst part of it? Without realizing it, we dressed Lil almost identically to the way her mother was dressed. It's a wonder Fury didn't have a heart attack. What were we thinking? But then it was so perfect for her. Martha, I sometimes forget that this little girl who is the center of our world is very definitely a gift to us from God. She shouldn't be here, my dear … if you only knew. Anyway, thanks to God's grace she is, and is loved beyond belief. This has been such a shock to Fury, he's really shaken up. In fact he's asked Bear if he could manage to stay up here for their honeymoon and then for Lil's birthday. He just doesn't feel comfortable having us without a man to protect us, and you know, of course I disagree, but I've never seen him quite like this." She paused and they looked at each other.

Martha put her hand over Raff's and said, "I think it's quite an honor for William-Bear. I imagine he would consider it a privilege."

Raff nodded. "Yes, he didn't even hesitate. Those two big men hugged each other, and it was a done deal. Billy Joe will go to Middleboro and take over the running of the lumberyard and come back for Lil's birthday. You all right with that?"

"Raff, I think it's perfect. Billy Joe can run the lumberyard with his eyes closed, and it will be good for his father to see that. I am delighted, as you know for many reasons." They hugged each other and Martha said, "I can hardly wait to read about our little girl."

Clay and I walked toward the small bunch clustered around Fury and Oatie.

Fury looked up and smiled at me. When I saw him smile, nothin' else mattered. I ran as fast as I could and he swooped me up into his arms. I nestled my head into my best spot, and my world was safe again.

He whispered into my ear, "How about this father having the next dance with his beautiful little daughter?"

I jerked my head up and put my finger on his nose. We looked at our eyes and I said, "I love you. You're my very best father and I love you."

I told Clay it was the best weddin' I'd ever been to.

He rolled his eyes and said, "Li-i-i-l, it's the *only* weddin' you've ever been to."

Clay danced most of the evenin' with Millie Jackson. I was covered up and layin' down on Martha's lap. I could barely keep my eyes open. I wanted to stay awake so's I could wave at my Mother and Father when they went on their honeymoon. Martha told me my father was gonna carry my Mother through our new front door. That sounded so silly I had to sit up. Martha and I got to laughin' so hard we couldn't stop and that was sure a highlight. We calmed down and I said, "What would happen if he dropped her?" That started us off again. We was so tired we was silly, but I surely loved it.

Mother and Father was the most beautiful dancers there. When I told them that, Uncle Bear did a lot of harrumphin', so I told him he and Raff would be the next best. They seemed content with that. They all decided to dance one more dance.

Clay came over and sat down and leaned his head against us. Martha ran her hand through his hair and said, "Have you had your fill, Clay? Did you outlast Millie, or did you both give up?"

He laughed and said, "Martha, I flat had my fill. I am plum tuckered out. I wish Mother and Father would get tired and go to 2-house. I get to stay with Bear and Runner and Pokey and the pups in their tent tonight. It'll be fun, but Uncle Bear says he's going to move us all into a Wet Walker cabin tomorrow 'cause the tent city is comin' down when the folks leave."

That woke me up a little and made me feel sad. I didn't want any of these folks to leave. Our home was so filled with happiness that I feared the emptiness when they left.

I struggled to sit up and tell Martha and Clay how bad I felt when the sounds in my ears all changed. The folks was laughin' and clappin' and hollerin' at Mother and Father. The last dance had ended, and they were holdin' hands and talkin' to everyone and headin' over to us.

Father picked me up and said, "You're almost sound asleep, little one, you need to hop in bed and have some sweet dreams."

He hugged and kissed me and put me in my Oatie Mother's arms. She loved me good and said, "Lil, you're our big girl and we're countin' on you to help out and keep these folks in line and keep everything runnin' smooth." She was so beautiful she took my breath away. I hugged her neck as hard as I could and told her that Clay and I would take care of everything. Unc-Father had Clay up in his arms and he didn't care how big he was. Clay was laughin' and huggin' him back.

They stood us together, and Clay grabbed my hand, and they held hands and ran for 2-house. The crowd was followin' 'em and it was so much fun. Martha had hold of our hands and Clay said, "Can we go watch – please, Martha?"

I looked up at her and said, "I sure don't want to miss that carryin' thing."

Martha laughed and started us walkin' towards 2-house. Father and Mother was up the porch stairs and had opened the front door.

Mary Smith

He cupped her face in his hands and kissed her good, and then – like she was light as a feather – he swept her up in his arms and carried her into the house. People yelled and hollered and it was my very best treasure for sure.

    … and he didn't drop her …

CHAPTER 9

I slept till that big ol' sun was clean up straight in the sky. I looked at Miss Myrtle and decided she's just a lazy child. She was still sound asleep. I didn't hear much noise even with the door open, but the little fire was hoppin' around in the fireplace like it wanted me to get up and dance. I felt my feet and they tingled when I touched 'em. I sure hope I didn't wear them out. I looked at 'em in the light that was shinin' through the door and I spied a little sore red spot. It made me remember. I had to stop and really wonder, was it real? Or was I just adreamin' it? I didn't have no, *any* shoes for a long time and I couldn't walk in our yard till the dew dried up. Then I 'membered my Mams drawin' my foot onto some tree bark and tyin' 'em on me. Then I 'membered when I got my beautiful yellow shoes and how good they felt and how I loved them, and then I 'membered yesterday. Yesterday I got grow'd up and got hi-button shoes. Everthin' that's happened since the barn-raisin' come rollin' back. I just plopped back down in my covers and looked at the pretty day outside.

Then I heard – what? Oh my, the creak of wagon wheels! What if I'd missed sayin' goodbye to all my new friends 'cause I was just a dumb sleepyhead. Oh no, please no. I jumped out of bed and went runnin' outside. Nobody was around the cook fire so I took off up the path to the tent town. People was everywhere laughin' and talkin' real easy-like as they was takin' down the tents. I saw Uncle Bear and Billy Joe gatherin' the tents up and stackin' 'em in a wagon. I ran into Uncle Bear and Runner's tent and found my Raff and my Martha. I was so out of breath, I could barely talk, but Martha grabbed a shawl and wrapped it around me and Raff stopped packin' things and just started laughin'. Runner was dressed and limpin' around with his big grin in place and Clay was on the floor pattin' Pokey and the Uglies.

Martha said, "Land sakes, Lil, you're runnin' around in your night dress. What are you thinking?"

I said, "I was thinkin' I didn't want to miss sayin' goodbye to my new friends."

Martha smiled and said, "Well, that would be a goodbye they wouldn't forget for a while. Raff, do you want to tend to this wild child or shall I?"

Raff got up off the floor, picked me up and said, "Go on with the packin' Martha, it'll be a lot easier on you than tacklin' this child who I assume is fully rested and full of energy. I'll get her cleaned up, fed, and back up here in the wink of an eye." She started toward the door with me, and I looked over her shoulder and waved my finger at Runner and Clay.

They was gigglin', and Clay said, "Hurry back, Lil, we've been savin' all the hard work for you."

I sure hoped he was funnin' with me. Raff was movin' right along, so I guess I'd soon find out.

While she was washin' and dressin' me, Raff was tellin' me what I missed last night when I konked out. "Now Lil," she said, "that's a silly word, so don't be usin' it or puttin' it in your melon."

Well, I felt bad she said that, cause I liked it a lot. KONKED out. It *was* silly, but it was a smiley word and maybe I'd 'member it and some day I could use it.

I had to try to get my words better, cause Raff had told me and Clay that things was about to change! She said our talkin' was downright sloppy and not to be tolerated. Whew. We were goin' to help set up a little schoolroom in one of the Wet Walker cabins and get to work learnin' somethin'. My Oatie-Mother was so gentle she'd let me go to sleep on her lap if I got tired of schoolin'. Raff saw us one day and told Oatie she was givin' her a vacation from teachin' us for a while. That she would be the schoolmarm till she got us back in shape. Clay and I had both sat up straight, with big eyes and reached for each other's hands.

After Raff went back to the box house, Oatie said, "You best work very hard for her. She's a strict taskmaster and if you slack even a little bit, you'll be doin' extra work. She used to tell me I was only fit to teach early first graders because she didn't think I could be firm enough to make anyone else learn. It will be hard, but you will be amazed at how much you'll know in a year. She loves teachin' and cookin' more than anything. Lil, this time next year, you'll be readin' books, real books, and you'll be starting to learn your first language – probably French. Clay, I know you've had a lot more schooling but I'm betting it's pretty rusty. With Raff in charge, it will come back quickly."

I loved listenin' to Raff. She had the best words I'd ever heard, and both my Father and Mother said she was so smart and had the best sense of anyone they knew. I also knew laziness was not acceptable. That's one of her favorite sayin's, and me and Clay know she means business!

Raff was still talkin' about last night and how everybody gathered around the fire and talked and sang. She said she would have worried about wakin' me up, except that she knew it would be humanly impossible. She also told me, by the way, that Mr. Clay fell sound asleep and Uncle Bear had to carry him to bed. So when he tells me how big he is and he stayed up with the big kids, I'll be able to put him in his place.

I wisht I could have stayed awake longer, but all my holes was filled and I just drifted off. I don't even 'member dreamin'.

She left me puttin' my yellow shoes on while she got my breakfast. She sat me down at our table, while she made up the bed and straightened our room. My weddin' dress was hangin' in the corner and I stopped eatin' and put my chin in my hand and just gazed at it.

It would always be my favorite dress and I'd never, ever forget it. Raff looked at me, then at the dress and said, "Lil, just like your Mother, you were the belle of the ball. I was very, very proud of you and Clay. It was such a fine time and such a beautiful memory. However, we don't have time for lollygaggin' right now because all your friends will be leaving. Margaret Faye and Preacher Jackson will stay on another night, but their children will be leaving soon, so we need to speed things up."

I started sittin' up straight and gettin' that food in, cause somethin' was tellin' me we was movin' right along. I was happy that we got finished on time, but I'm thinkin' my tummy might be wonderin' how come I didn't chew my food!

When we got back to tent town, it was almost gone. I felt so sad. I didn't realize how it had become a part of our lives. I was seein' some of the little white rocks that had been searched for and painted white and placed to show where all those tents would be. They looked so worn and useless and like no one cared about them any more.

Raff was standin' by me and, as usual, she seemed to know what I was thinkin'. She said, "You know Lil, I've been thinking. All these wonderful little white rocks need not be wasted. I believe they would be just right to outline this whole upper pasture, and now that we have a real road, thanks to the wagons, it sure seems like it would be fine if they were to outline and border it on each side. If we don't have enough, we can always find some more and outline all our pathways to the box house and 2-house and the cabins. It certainly would make a much neater appearance. What do you think?"

I was all but jumpin' up and down. I said, "Oh Raff, that would be the prettiest thing in the world. I vowed to never pick up another rock, but I will, I will, I'll search for 'em and help paint 'em and put 'em out. Oh, wouldn't that be the prettiest thing?"

Raff said, "The prettiest thing, Lil, is the way your eyes are dancin' and your willingness to help. I'll bring it up to Bear and Billy Joe and get their viewpoint so that when Fury comes back, we'll have a plan."

I clapped and jumped and said, "Can I go tell Martha and Clay and Runner what you've thought of? I know they'll be excited!"

I couldn't wait to get in the tent and tell 'em. They was almost through packin', and they all thought it was a grand idea. There wasn't much left in the tent except the doggy box. I dared look over to it and there was that Pokey girl just a waggin' her tail like she'd been waitin' for me. She melted my heart. I reminded myself that I was doin' better and that I needed to go look at the Uglies. Clay was layin' by 'em like he loved 'em to pieces, and I thought he deserved both of the puppies. Then I looked at 'em. They weren't the same rat things. They were covered with soft silky hair like their mother, and their little eyes was open. One was brown and white and the other was black and white. Little Pokey leaned towards 'em and licked 'em, and they squealed.

Clay said, "Be careful, Lil, your eyes are gonna pop out of your head!"

I didn't pay him any mind, I just got on my knees by the box and started goin' oooohoohoooh. One of the little things, the little fat brown and white one, tried to wiggle towards my fingers. Martha and Raff was behind me and I was so overcome, I could hardly talk.

Martha said, "Lil, that baby is trying to get to you. It hears your sounds and is trying to find you. Touch it and see what it does."

I very carefully extended my fingers to touch it and it was so silky. I moved my fingers very gently and it kept wigglin' till its wee pink nose touched 'em. When it finally did, it jerkily raised its little head and then laid down, touchin' my finger, and gave a little sigh. Almost like it knew it was home and safe. I just loved it. I don't know what happened to those ugly little rats, but this baby was precious and she would grow up to be just like Pokey, and she was mine. I looked up into the faces of Martha and Raff and then at Clay and quietly said, "I'd like to have this one if I may, I'd like to have this one for my very own, and I'll call her Lacy." Clay almost jumped for joy and he and Runner ran out the door.

Martha said, "They went to tell Bear and Billy Joe that you didn't pick his dog. He has been scared silly that you'd choose the black and white one. He is a true little gentleman, Lil. We asked him what he'd do if you did and he looked so stricken we were ashamed of ourselves. He looked us straight in the eye and made us promise never to tell you. He said he'd given his word, and he would not go back on it, especially to you!"

I took my other hand and gently rubbed the little thing. It seemed to love it and turned its little head back and forth and squealed and squeaked. "Could I …?"

"Tomorrow," Raff said. "Lil, when you leave them, always tuck them in close to their mother's tummy. That way they can get a little milk and go to sleep and be safe in Pokey's arms."

When she said Pokey, her tail started waggin' and her eyes was glued on mine, almost like she was askin' me to love her puppy. I scratched under her chin and rubbed her head and back. She tried to lick me, so I put my hand near her mouth and, sure enough, out came that little rough tongue and she licked and licked.

Martha said, "Well, this has been quite a day, I'd say. No one can ever doubt when you're happy Lil. Your eyes shine like nothing I've ever seen. If I was your beau, I'd probably say 'they shine like stars in the heavens above!'" She hugged me and said, "When Clay and Runner come back, we'll be ready to move them into a Wet-Watcher cabin."

I said, "Let me go find him, Martha. Raff, can I tell him about the rocks?" She nodded her head, and I was almost out the door when I stopped and went back for one more look at Lacy. She was fat and already asleep and she was precious and she was my very best treasure.

We said goodbye to our friends on the wagons. Ever'one said they'd see us in the spring. It was fun 'cause with all that hard work they were happy and had a wonderful time.

Raff said, "That's the way of good people, Lil. We're very fortunate that your Father, Fury, spent time in Middleboro and got to know so many good people."

I said, "Raff, how long are Mother and Father gonna have to stay in 2-house by themselves? I bet they're missin' all of us. Don't you think they'd be hungry by now? If they stay a whole week, they won't be able to come out 'cause they'll have starved to death. I think we should go rescue them. I bet they'd be glad and mighty proud of us and I could show them Lacy. Think of all they're missin'. I bet they'll be mad."

Raff said, "Well, Lil, you'll not win this round. They definitely won't be a bit mad. They are enjoying each other and firming up plans for their family's lives. That's you, and Clay too. They've undertaken a huge project, plus two wonderful children. That's a mighty large responsibility. No, I believe they'll be very happy if we just tend to our business and see that everything runs smoothly till they choose to return to us."

I said, "What if they decide never to come out?"

"LiL, that's enough." Raff said, pretending to be put out with me. Martha was laughin' and I giggled and before long us wimmin was havin' us a real good time.

We got all our new livin' quarters put together. The cabin they chose would be Runner's cabin. For now, Uncle Bear and Clay would be there with him. He was gettin' stronger and he never stopped smilin', but we all knew he wasn't just sore on the outside. He was cheerful and he tried to work himself to death seemed like. Soon as our folks came out (if they ever did), then Clay and I and Miss Myrtle and Lacy and Barney would all move into 2-house. Raff and Martha chose to stay in our box house. There was an extra window tucked in the storage area meant for it, and Uncle Bear and Billy Joe were goin' to put it in before Billy Joe went to Middleboro. Uncle Bear and Father were goin' to put it in later, but Billy Joe convinced them that it was foolish to wait 'cause he'd installed many a window. If they got it done today, then everyone could start gettin' their quarters arranged to suit 'em. Raff and Martha was all for that, in fact they both were almost silly about it. I was thinkin' it was just a dumb old window, and then I 'membered how my little Mam had loved hers and how I loved all the windows in 2-house.

The men was takin' sawdust and brooms and was sweepin' our property. They were all tryin' to get the hardest work done before Billy Joe left, because Uncle Bear didn't want Runner left thinkin' he wasn't doin' enough. Clay and I would gather the white rocks into a pile, and then we'd take our new wagons that were made for us by the Preacher's kids and go rock searchin' again. Everyone loved Raff's idea of white-rockin' our place, so Clay and I couldn't wait to start addin' to our rock pile.

Raff and Martha had picked out our schoolroom, and Billy Joe knew where there was a bunch of old desks stashed in the old abandoned school house in Middleboro. He said some of them weren't in good shape, but he'd see if he couldn't do some repairs, and he'd bring 'em up when he come for my birthday. Ever'one was excited and lookin' forward to my birthday. I couldn't imagine why. It just seemed like it would be another day. I knew it sure wasn't gonna be like a weddin', and I just couldn't get my melon excited. Clay kept sayin' that dumb "you'll see" till I wanted to bang him with a broom! I was so glad all the Jackson's were comin' for my birthday. Raff and Martha kept explainin' how this was to be a celebration of my birth. It would be a joyous occasion and I tried to make my eyes dance like they was always talkin' about but nothin' seemed to happen.

Clay said, "Lil, when anyone mentions your birthday, you look like need a nap. What's wrong with you? You'll just love it! See, you're just lookin' at me like you wish I'd hurry up and finish talkin' about it, so we could go have fun. Everyone will think you don't care."

I said, "Clay, I love everybody and I don't want to make anybody feel bad, but I'm guessin' I don't care, cause I've never seen a birthday or heard anybody havin' one. I can't seem to make my eyes sparkle for 'em, and I'm worried I'll be a disappointment."

Raff heard the last of our talkin'. She walked over and gathered both of us and said, "I think the two of you need to stop worryin' about Lil's birthday. It'll be more fun if it's a surprise. We're gonna get her so worried she may have one of her fits or get sour on us."

I looked at her eyes real quick and they was twinklin', so I knew she was just funnin'.

She went on, "There's so much to do around here, we're all going to be up to our ears in work. Bear says he'd like you two to ride with him to send Billy Joe off tomorrow, so let's get busy and get lots done before the sun goes down. You both need to go feed your animals, bring the eggs back, go see your puppies, and then report back to me. And ... make it snappy." She grinned, because she knew I'd love that new sayin' and she was right.

That evenin' when we were all sittin' around the cook stove eatin' together, tired from a good workin' day, everyone was chattin' about all sorts of things, and we were all watchin' the smoke curl from the chimney in 2-house. It was so pretty weavin' around the trees in the twilight and smellin' so good.

Uncle Bear said, "I loaded them up with almond wood to burn because of that fragrance. It's the best burner, but it's that wonderful smell that always gets me."

We all heard it at the same time. The haunting sound of a violin. Unc-Father was playin' his love songs to our Mother. Ever'one had tears in their eyes and that music made me swell inside till I thought I'd burst. Oh I loved it. Raff and Martha, sittin' side by side, looked at each other and started singin'. I don't have the good words to tell how these wimmin sound when they sing, but it's like God-Willin's angels had crawled inside of them. They sang till darkness came and we were all soothed and ready for bed.

Martha looked at Uncle Bear and Billy Joe and said, "I wish for my piano. I'd like to give it to Lil and teach her how to play it before ... before she gets any older." I was watchin' her, then I looked at everyone else and I knew somethin', some kind of secret was afoot, but I didn't know what. I was dizzy with the thought of a piano, but I had no idea what it was. I knew what violins, banjos, gee-tars, and acordy-on boxes were like, but I didn't know how to picture a piano.

Billy Joe did a lot of throat clearin' and looked at his father. Uncle Bear was lookin' directly at Martha. He said, "Let me see if I understand this correctly. I am feelin' that you are planning on remaining up here – permanently? Is that what you want, my dear? You know how much we love you and want only your happiness. I also want you safe and comfortable. Martha, there is no doctor up here, as you know."

Martha did a sweepin' brush with her hand and said, "William, we both know I no longer have any need of a doctor. I am alone in Middleboro. You and Billy Joe are gone much of the time, and it's left to my friends to make extra effort in their busy days to look out for me. Here, I'm never alone. I feel I can be of help again. There's a meaning to my life. These people and little Lil have given me a reason to be. I know you and Billy Joe well enough to know you both feel strongly enough about Wet Walkers that you are going to be up here more and more, so I guess, yes, I want to remain up here. I am happy, peaceful and inspired. To teach Lil piano gives me a purpose and some meaning to life again."

Tears was runnin' down my wonderful Billy Joe's face, and he got up and went to his mother. He put his arms around her with his head next to hers.

She patted him and said, "I know you and your father understand, my darlin', so I am making a list of things I'd like you to bring – and the piano, if you can manage it. Since the Jackson family will be coming up at the same time, you'll have plenty of help. Now, let's consider this a celebration, because I feel all this happiness has given me an extension. Does everyone feel all right about my decision?"

Everyone mumbled words like – 'of course, whatever makes you happy' and on and on. Clay and I was sittin' like sticks watchin' all these grownups sayin' and doin' stuff and wonderin' what it meant. We was holdin' hands as tight as we could, and I had the feelin' my eyes was about to pop out of my head. I just knew I was right. Our mother and father needed to come out of 2-house. There was too much they was missin'. I didn't know what it all meant, but I knew Martha was gonna be a part of our family forever, and

… a piano was comin' …

CHAPTER 10

Raff says, "Busy people don't get into mischief."

Well, Clay and I surely know how true that is. Time has been flyin' by. Runner has almost made a whole mountain of rocks all by himself.

Clay and I looked at each other in confusion. He said, "Am I a slowpoke, Lil, or are you?"

I said, "Clay, I'm thinkin' we're both slowpokes."

When Runner heard us say that, he just laughed and laughed and laughed, jumped up and down and seemed so full of energy that we're thinkin' he's back to his old self.

We rode with Billy Joe to the fork in the road. He got off his horse and came over and lifted me off Dancer's back and he hugged me and whispered in my ear, "Watch over Martha for me, darlin', she sure does love you."

I said, "I love her too, Billy Joe, we'll all take care of her. I sure wish you wasn't goin'."

"Hey, what's that look for? I'll be back before you have time to miss me!"

I knew that wasn't so, but I tried to put on a happy face anyway.

Instead of headin' right home, Uncle Bear took Clay and me on a long leisurely ride in the mountains surroundin' our Wet Walker compound. I never, ever dreamed these trails and all this prettiness was so close to us. A long time ago, when my Oatie and Raff Mams took me tree cuttin', I saw magical things, but what we were seein' was more than my ten fingers. I caught my breath so many times Clay got worried for fear I'd end up with a mouthful of bugs. Dancer was lovin' just moseyin' along.

When Uncle Bear walked us under a waterfall, we was all thrilled, but I was scared. I felt my Dancer's skin ripple over and over, so I knew she was nervous too. We saw a rainbow and it hadn't even rained. I said that to Uncle Bear.

He pushed his hat back, scratched his head and said, "Well sweetheart, I reckon it's raining somewhere."

When we got home, we were so tired we almost fell off our horses. Even Dancer's little head was down. We told Uncle Bear we'd walk 'em to the stream and let 'em get a good drink before we brushed 'em and put 'em to bed. He nodded and rode on down to the corral.

Clay said, "He's down, Lil, he's sad that Martha will stay up here. I think there's a lot we don't know. Somethin's making him awful blue."

When we got down to the corral, Uncle Bear had his horse tended to and most of the animals fed. He talked to 'em and made 'em all happy. He did everything so easy, nothin' seemed to be hard work for him. When we walked into the barn to brush our horses he said, "Lil, we need to be getting you a saddle. I don't know what I was thinkin' of to ride you all over tarnation when you had nothing to hang on to 'cept a halter. Martha'd have my scalp. It's a pure wonder you didn't slide right off-a Dancer's back when we climbed some of those little hills. Fury'd skin me alive."

I said, "Uncle Bear, we was just moseyin' along and Uncle Fury, Father taught me to wrap my fists all tight in her mane. Once I didn't have as good a hold as I should have, and she just stopped and got sideways, so I could get a better grip."

Clay said, "It's true, Uncle Bear, I was behind her the whole time. She and Dancer have each other figured out pretty good, and she seemed fine."

"Good God a'Mighty," Uncle Bear bellered, "I must have been out of my mind! You'll not be riding her again till we get you a saddle."

I burst out crying. I didn't know what I'd done wrong or why I'd upset him. If I couldn't ride my Dancer, it would, it would break my heart. She was nuzzlin' me, and I put my head into her neck. She knew I was sad and didn't have arms to wrap me in, so I put my arms around her and sobbed. Willy and Nelly came bouncin' up and tried to lick me and stop me hurtin'. Leggs was a brayin' and saunterin' towards me.

"My God, what's going on with these animals? Get back there, Leggs." Leggs just kept headin' for me.

Clay said, "Uncle Bear, these are Lil's animals. They've been hers from when she started her livin'. They love her and they don't want her upset. Please tell us what's wrong, Uncle Bear. Don't make Lil cry like this. What have we done to upset you?" Clay was cryin' too.

The door to the barn opened and Raff came in. She said, "Well, this is a fine kettle of fish. What on God's earth is goin' on? Thank goodness, I made Martha go in the box house and rest a bit. What has upset these animals like this? Lil, are you crying? Come here, child, and Clay. What is going on, William? You've got both of the children crying, and the animals sound like they're going on a rampage. Let go of Dancer, honey, she's fine." I let her pick me up and Clay was clutchin' her skirts. She said, "I'm waiting."

Uncle Bear pulled his hat off and went to one of the benches in front of the stalls. He put his head into his hands and sobbed huge giant sobs. He said, "I'm half crazy, Raff. I'm not thinkin' straight and I led these children on a ride that could have hurt them, and I didn't even look back to check them I was so lost in my own thoughts. Oh my God, what am I going to do? I was so stunned at what I'd done, I told Lil she wasn't to ride Dancer again till she got a saddle. My God, Raff."

She interrupted and said simply, "William, stop taking the Lord's name in vain. You'll get no help from Him by doing that."

Uncle Bear calmed down and said, "Raff, she rode for two, three hours over somewhat treacherous and precarious territory without me even glancin' back."

Raff said, "Well William, for starters, Lil's part horse. When a child not yet five has the gift that Lil has with animals, it's best to leave our human hands off of her. Like it or not, I would venture to say she has more knowledge and sense about animals than you or I. Clay is responsible and was guarding her. That being said, yes, it was unconscionable that you behaved in that manner; however, what's done is done and no ill has come from it. Stop crying, Lil, and you too, Clay. Uncle Bear's not himself. He's upset and we need to talk. You two are fine, and he said what he did about you not riding Dancer because he loves you and was upset that he might have caused you harm.

"You both heard Martha tell us all of her decision to remain here this morning. You know she's sick. You just don't know that she's very, very sick. I will take care of her and we will all love her to pieces …" her voice broke "… for as long as she lives.

"Now, that having been said, let's all pull together and make this time as good and happy as we can. I was making soup for our supper and have a loaf of bread in the oven. I want you two to scamper up there and stir the soup and take charge of supper. Can you do that?"

We both nodded and she said, "Then get along with you. William and I will have a chat and then we'll be up. All right?"

We both looked shyly at Uncle Bear and without hesitation went to him, threw our arms around him and smothered him with kisses, tellin' him we loved him. He started blubberin' again, and Raff said, "Good grief, run on or you'll get him started again, and I'll never get him stopped. And not a word to Martha, do you understand?"

We nodded and both ran for the door and headed for the cook fire.

Raff walked over to William's dejected figure, his head in his hands. She said, "Well, you certainly earned your nickname, Uncle Bear!"

He looked up at her sheepishly and stood finally. He put his arms around her and said, "Raff…"

"Hush William, Bear, whoever you are. This is a difficult time." He kissed her with such love that they both faltered. She said, "William, you know that Martha and I formed an instant bond when we met. I am closer to her than Oatie. I doubt very much that you knew she was searching desperately to find someone to care for her family. She says she knew it was me the minute she laid eyes on me. Weeks later, when she almost didn't live through the night, she asked me, then made me promise, that I would take care of you and watch over Billy Joe till he married. I have to admit I would have promised her anything. As time went on, she has been contented because of that promise. The only hitch is, I had no intention of falling in love with you." He started to say something, but she put her fingers on his lips. "Sssh, William, hear me out. I won't say this again. Loving you has restored my life and heart, but my friend came first. I knew I had to be honest with her." William gasped, she went on, "I told her of my feelings that have developed for you." Tears streamed from her eyes, and she said, "'My cup runneth over.' She knows of our love and rejoices in it. You and I are who we are, and to each of us – she will come first. Now, my love, let's be grateful for one another and cherish our love, but keep it in perspective. All your moping and hating Martha's heart condition won't make it better, so waste no more precious time on that. I honestly think she made that announcement this morning to nudge you into moving up here. I'm sure Billy Joe can run the lumberyard blindfolded and you know we'll be needin' you with all that's coming. It's your decision, however, and we'll honor it."

"Raff," William said, "I love you so very much."

"And I you, my dearest William. Now, let's go tend to our other loved ones. Shall we?"

CHAPTER 11

It was already Saturday, and that meant our Mother and Father would join us tomorrow. Clay and I could hardly wait. We'd be movin' into 2-house. Clay, of course, knew what it would be like, but I was havin' some sorry thoughts. What if I got lost, or stuck someplace little, or caught on something, or who knows what?

The sun was out full, and we were sittin' outside havin' us a picnic lunch of sorts when I saw Clay's eyes get so big they about popped out. Raff was sittin' next to him and she burst into laughter. Uncle Bear and I turned around just as Martha and Runner looked up and there was Uncle Fury and Oatie, my Mother and Father. I couldn't help it, I screamed and jumped up and ran into their arms. Clay was right behind me. We was jumpin' up and down and hollerin'.

Raff threw her arms around them and said, "Welcome back to the real world. We've certainly missed you."

I said, "I bet you're about starved to death and smelled the good food and knew you had to come get some. I told Raff over and over we needed to come get you, but she wouldn't let me, and I prayed God-Willin' wouldn't let you starve to death cause Raff wouldn't let me come save you."

I was in Oatie's arms and she'd about kissed me to pieces and she felt pretty strong, and I felt stronger arms takin' me from her and I was safe in my Father's arms. I couldn't help it, I started sobbin' into his neck. Oh, I loved my Mam and Pap. I squeezed him so hard I thought I'd surely bust his neck, but he just kept dancin' around hummin' to me and tellin' me he loved me, and how they'd talked about me and Clay, and how they'd missed us. Oh, he smelled so good, I'd never get enough. They hugged and kissed everyone, and it was the best time.

They asked Runner all sorts of questions like, was he happy, did he like his house, and he liked to had a fit. He was bouncin' and turnin' while he was talkin' and seemed to cover the whole week's happenin's in three bounces. They were excited to see Pokey and the pups. My Oatie Mam said she loved the name Lacy and couldn't wait to see 'em.

Uncle Fury said, "Clay, wherever did you get the name Barney from? They're both girls, aren't they?

Clay looked sheepish and said, "It's my first very own dog and I wanted to remember always when I got her. It was … er, ah … well, it was at the barn-raisin', hoedown time."

Uncle Fury said, "So, barn-raisin' became Barney, right?" Clay nodded and Uncle Fury continued, "Well, son, if you and Barney are happy with that name, it's fine with us and if you decide to change it, we'll all put our heads together. How's that sound?"

Clay beamed and looked at me. We had missed our parents somethin' awful and ever'one knew it. Especially them. Uncle Fury didn't act like he would ever set me down, and I was so glad. I wanted him to hold on to me forever. They looked so happy and beautiful. I was glad they was our Mother and Father, or Mam and Pap, or Uncle Fury and Oatie, or whoever. They were ours and they were the best.

Uncle Bear and Martha beamed at them and Uncle Bear said, "Welcome home, it's about by-God (he looked at Raff who frowned), it's about by-Gosh time." He looked at Martha and said, "That sounds downright dumb." She raised her eyebrows and giggled.

Uncle Fury whooped and said, "Sounds like Raff's gotten to you, too, Bear. We'll have to have us a poker and cigar evenin' occasionally so we can cuss a little."

They both laughed and Raff, Oatie and Martha looked put out, but the corners of their mouths was twitchin'. Oh, how I loved my family bein' back and all of us bein' so happy again.

All of a sudden, everyone was talkin' at once and laughin' and it was back to the "good ol' times." That's a Martha sayin', and I love it.

When lunch was over, Oatie said, "We thought perhaps we'd let the children sleep in their new beds tonight. We also thought it might be fun, now that the evenings are getting cooler, if we all ate dinner around our dinner table. It will be my first dinner party and I can't wait. What do you think?" Everyone was excited and said so.

Raff said, "Well, for our first dinner in 2-house we'll not be havin' leftover soup and corn bread. I'll make a ham loaf and put some dried corn to soakin' and the children can pick us a bucket of spinach greens. I've got jars of canned cherries and, although Lil and Martha usually tend to the pastries, I'll whip up a quick pie. I already have two loaves of rye bread raising, so we'll have a little feast. After all, this is a real celebration. Runner, can you and Clay clean up this lunch mess for us, so we can start getting things together ready for the move?"

Runner and Clay hopped up and had things straightened up almost before we'd walked to the box house.

Raff, said, "My lands, I've been wasting my precious time! These young men can work circles around me. What on earth have I been thinking?"

Runner and Clay looked real proud and turned a little pink and I giggled.

Uncle Fury turned his head to my cheek and said quiet-like, "What are you gigglin' about, Lil?"

I whispered to him, "I get tickled when their faces turn pink." He grinned and I said, "Uncle Fury, I'm not ready in my head or my mouth to call you and my Oatie Mam those big Mother and Father names. My heart knows you're my Mother and Father, but it hasn't got to my mouth yet. I just love callin' you whatever comes out. I'm workin' so hard tryin' to get it right that it's makin' my head and mouth both hurt. Will that make you feel sad? Will it seem like I don't want you to be my Mother and Father? I've just worried and worried, and I thought you'd never come out of 2-house and be my Pap and my Oatie Mam. I don't ever want you to go away again. I don't want you to get married no, *any* more and I sure don't want no more honeymoon weeks."

He was holdin' me so tight I could barely breathe. He walked over and sat on a log and sat me on his lap, so I was part facin' him. He had tears drippin', he wiped 'em away and said, "Little dear heart, you will never, ever know, even when you're all grown up, how dearly your Oatie Mam and I love you. You are the joy of our world. You and Clay make our life worth living. We don't care what you call us, precious child. We'll know you're sayin' what your heart feels. Don't worry any more, Lil, I sure don't want to raise a worry wart!"

I laughed and clapped. My Mam and Pap was back and my insides was so happy they was dancin'.

We was walkin' up the steps to 2-house and was all excited 'cause it's the first time we saw it dressed. I didn't know what to expect. I was more excited to see the chair Uncle Fury and Uncle Bear was gonna make outta their arms to carry Martha up to the 2-house. They all said my eyes was dancin'. Oatie Mam said she worried a little when she saw that, because she'd decided it might be a forerunner of a mischievous act.

I was thinkin' to put those words in my melon, but they were too big to fit. But someday I'll know them, those words, next time I hear 'em, and I'll know what they mean. My mouth just isn't ready yet.

Walkin' through that door was so scary I thought I'd surely faint. I'd never seen a house other than our little box house. I got all excited when we got beds and chairs and tables for the Wet Walker cabins. They was almost too much for me to think about. I'd been hearin' about the wagonloads of furchur, household goods, that would be goin' into 2-house, but none of those words said anythin' that I knew about. I knew all about my colors and my numbers and my animals and good food and shoes and my dresses and my doll and simple things. Seems like I had an awful lot of things I knew about, but I guess I wasn't ready for what my eyes saw when we opened the door to 2-house. Clay and I had been talkin' about it, and I was happy and excited – cause he was. All those new things he talked about sounded like such fun. I didn't know in my head what none of 'em looked like, so he just kept tellin' me things cause he was lovin' watchin' my mouth fall open.

When that door opened, no one laughed. It scared me so bad that I knew I'd have nightmares for the rest of my life. I started cryin' so hard I couldn't stop, and even Uncle Fury's safe place didn't help. He told people to go on in and he'd walk me a little. I just sobbed and sobbed and I didn't even know why. He didn't try to stop me. He hummed and rubbed my back and walked up to my gentle little stream. He sat down on the big rock and nuzzled my neck, kissin' me, but just kept hummin'. I sobbed till there wasn't nuthin' left, my tears was all out, and the hiccups started. He patted my curls and rocked me. He finally got his hanky out of his pocket and blew my nose and wiped me up as best he could. I slid my eyes to his, but they was frowny eyes, not happy ones, and he didn't even look at me. He didn't say nuthin' and when I quieted down, I got to wonderin' why.

Finally I couldn't stand it, and I said, "Uncle Fury?"

He quietly said, "Yes, Lil?"

I didn't exactly know what to say and he wasn't sayin' anythin'. I figgered this was all my doin', so I guessed he was waitin' for me to fix it. I just didn't know how. I said, "Uncle Fury, why'd I do that? My insides is still shiverin'." I pulled back so's I could look at his face and at his eyes.

He finally looked right into my eyes and said, "Because you're a very little girl and you've had so many new things happen to you in a year's time that you just weren't ready to see anything else. Lil, grownups forget what it's like to be a child. We think we don't, but we do. We grow up adjusting to things because changes usually come easily. If they don't, it can be very hard on a little one, and they get scared and feel alone and they stop feeling safe. Lots of parents rush right on, cause we figure you'll catch up, but Lil, sometimes little ones don't, and that's our fault. You see, darlin', God has given me a second chance at happiness that I never believed I'd have or deserve and you're a very large part of that. Are you understanding all these words I'm saying? Do I need to go slower? Would you rather just sleep or rest for a while? You tell me, so we'll get this right."

I said, "You talk to me good, Uncle Fury. I've let everyone I love down again. You seem to know why, and you're not mad or disappointed in me and I'm so happy. When I was cryin' and couldn't get stopped, I figerred the only thing I could do was run away, but Uncle Fury, I don't even know how to do that. I kept thinkin' I'd put on my yellow shoes and my overalls, but how would I carry my pretty dresses and my hi-button shoes? I could take Miss Myrtle and lead Dancer, but how could I take Lacy or Leggs or Willy or Nelly? I got scared inside of goin' and leavin' ever'one and everthin' I love, or stayin' and being sad and makin' 'em all unhappy."

Uncle Fury put his arms clear around me and hugged and rocked me. He said, "Oh Lil, the only thing I can think of that would make every one of us sad and unhappy would be if we didn't have you. While we're here together by our wonderful little fishing stream, let me be real easy and point out all the things your little girl, but very smart, mind has already accepted without you knowing it. Shall I do that for you, Lil?"

I said, "Oh yes please, Uncle Fury, please."

He said, "Close your eyes, Lil, so your mind can show you pictures. First, there's all of your animals – just think of each and every one of them, you better include mine and Clay's and Billy Joe's too. That's a lot of animals to enjoy, isn't it?"

I nodded and he went on, "Think about loving your Oatie and Raff Mams and your own memories of your little Mam and Pap, then start adding all the people in your life that you've met and enjoy and even love, AND all the things and happenings big and little that knowing them has brought to you. That's a LOT of things. Then look around you with your eyes closed – and see where and how you live. All the white rocks, all of our wonderful buildings and the school/meeting house to come, and who knows what else? That's a lot of things. Then look at your garden. All of the wonderful vegetables and foodstuffs Oatie and Raff have grown for you and even taught you how. That's really a lot."

I said, "Uncle Fury? Can we go back? I want to be with my family and see what new things I'm gonna have and know about. I want to go back, Uncle Fury, right now, so we don't miss nuthin', anythin' that I'm goin' to have and know about. Hurry, Uncle Fury, hurry, or we'll miss somethin'."

He kissed me, smiled and said, "Would you like a horseback ride back to the house?"

I said, "Uncle Fury I'm almost five years old, I'm gettin' too big for that."

He grinned, turned around and said, "All right then, let's hurry before you're five."

I laughed and laughed, and we went ridin' back to 2-house.

I could hear my family inside talkin' and laughin'. They left that front door open so we could walk in. I slid down off my horse, grabbed his hand and once again walked up the steps. I had some shy lumps inside, but these was my family who loved me and I had hold of Uncle Fury's hand. I looked up at him.

He smiled and said, "It's all right, Lil, they still love you."

I looked all around and at their smilin' faces and I was so glad these folks was my family.

Oatie Mam came up to me, gave me a hug and kiss, took my hand and said, "I'll give you a catch-up walk through the downstairs and then Fury and Uncle Bear will make a chair for our darlin' Martha and carry her upstairs. I know you'll just love seein' that.

It wasn't near as frightenin' as I thought, and the furchur was so pretty and it didn't scare me a bit. I couldn't wait to eat at our great big table with my very own chair, but I REALLY couldn't wait to see Martha go up the stairs!

Those two big men did their arms funny and they knelt down and Oatie and Raff helped her sit on the seat they'd made and they stood up and up they went. Clay put my hand on the rail and climbed slowly behind me and Martha was sittin' down laughin' by the time we got up there. It was wonderful and I wisht we could do it again. I loved all of it and there were rugs-blanket things on the floor so you could hear steps and then none. This was the biggest bunch of things I ever had, but I was gettin' used to lots of things. We went in my room first and I had my very own bed. I got goosey cause I was used to sleepin' in the big bed with Oatie and Raff and Miss Myrtle. Then I thought, I'll still sleep with Miss Myrtle and maybe Lacy can even crawl in with me. I saw a little seat in front of somethin' that was holdin' a mirror. I couldn't say a word. I clutched Oatie's hand and looked up at her. I couldn't believe it.

She said, "Yes, Lil, that's your very own mirror. You can see your little Mam every day so you'll never forget her. I wanted it to be for your birthday, but your Uncle Fury, well, he just couldn't wait."

"Kin I climb up on that little stool and look?"

"Yes Lil, you *MAY.*"

I meant may I, I'm just not thinkin' good. But I climbed right up and looked in the mirror and there she was. There she was. She looked like she'd been cryin' and her nose was all red, but I smiled at her big as I could and she smiled right back at me and there was her dimple and I could feel mine too. She'd always be in my room with me! Oh, this was my best treasure ever.

The rest of the house was a blur, but I knew our 2-house was beautiful and I'd be growin' up in it, so I was glad I really loved it. My room had a painted box with drawers. Martha pulled one out and there were my overalls. She explained that all my clothes was in there. There was a tall box with doors that was painted like the drawer box. She opened the doors and there were my dresses hangin' and my hi-button shoes sittin' on the bottom. It was my very own clothes-press and the drawer box was a dresser. I had my window seat and a real chair that was covered in material. It was soft and cozy.

I didn't know what it was for, but Martha pointed to the candlestick on the table beside the chair and said, "I imagine the time will soon come when you'll be reading books and won't want to quit just cause it's dark. Did you see your little bookcase, Lil?"

She pointed to a wall by the door and there was a dear little box with two shelves. It had real books in it. I gasped. They were to be mine? Oh I could hardly stand it.

Raff said, "Right now, they are mostly readers for school and learning, but I'm sure knowing your Martha and fa—Uncle Fury will be building book cases in your room! Everyone chuckled, and I clapped and danced around the room.

Clay caught hold of my hands and we danced a jig. He said, "Come see my room, Lil." We went runnin' in to see his room. It sure wasn't pretty like my room, but I didn't tell him that and it seemed like he thought it was, so I just kept my mouth shut!

Everythin' was wonderful and when Miss Martha got her ride downstairs, Clay and I took hold of the banisters and went down the stairs. The steps was so big I had to step down and put my other foot beside it before I could take another step, so it took me longer.

I was thinkin' of sittin' down and slidin', but Uncle Fury had been watchin' me and seemed to know what I was thinkin'. He said, "Don't ever take chances on the stairway, Lil. Take your time, go slowly and do it right. It can be dangerous, so we all need to be very careful." He knitted his eyebrows and looked sternly at Clay, who turned bright red. Fury said, "That's right, Clay, I'm glad you haven't forgotten your experience. Mr. Clay got too big for his britches when he was a little tyke about your age and decided he could run down those steps. Do you want to tell Lil how that worked out?"

Clay looked at me with a sheepish grin and pulled his hair back and showed me where he had a big cut on his forehead. I gasped and he nodded. "There was blood everywhere and I was in bed for a week. I fell all the way down the stairs, it hurt something fierce and scared the living daylights out of me."

I thought I'd always be careful of those stairs and never be an idjit on 'em, but I'd just heard a bunch of new sayin's and needed to get 'em in my melon!

That night we had dinner together at our family table. We each had our very own chair. I felt so grow'd, grown up, like I was already five. They had to put two pillows on my chair for me to reach the tabletop, but it was such fun. The food seemed to taste better, and we had plates that would break if you dropped 'em, and gre-e-e-at big snowy white (tho I'd never seen snow), that's what Martha called 'em, mouth wipes that's called nap-kins now. A glass glass to drink water out of and ... silverware that shined so brightly they were like a mirror. I could see my nose in my spoon! Clay and I got to cuttin' up and laughin' so hard we got close to bein' bawled out and reminded that anyone without table manners was likely to be found eatin' alone in the kitchen! I felt awful, but I still didn't dare look at Clay.

They held their glasses up and said, "Here's to Lil's birthday."

I felt pretty big and plenty proud. Two days till I was five. The piano was comin' up tomorrow with Billy Joe and a bunch of other things Raff ordered to cook for the celebration like roast beef – yum – and things that were secret. Margaret Faye and the Preacher was comin' tomorrow, so it was beginnin' to sound like I might *really* like birthdays. I couldn't think beyond the piano.

After dinner, Uncle Fury opened those big doors and tuned up his violin. He said, "I have been informed by Martha and others that you, Lil, are to receive a beautiful piano for your birthday. Somehow, I can't think of a more befitting and wonderful gift; but I, your humble servant, have only a small talent to offer you – but it's from my heart."

He lifted the violin to his chin and played our beautiful song in a way I'd never heard it. I thought if they hadn't tied me in my chair with a big sash, I'd surely fall on the floor in a heap.

CHAPTER 12

When I opened my eyes, I thought I was still dreamin'. I'm in a garden of flowers. It's beautiful and smells even better. I sneaked my fingers up to touch my eyes and ... they was open ... I was awake. Miss Myrtle was in my arms, sound asleep, and I felt like I was driftin' on a cloud. My head was on three down pillows and I had snowy-white pillows and linens. They smelled like the out of doors after a rain, and lavender. I have a down comfort to cover me with, and I was ready to go back to sleep all day.

    I could hear gentle people sounds, cause my door was half open. Then I could hear tap, tap, tap as someone came up those steps. Even bein' nosy didn't make me think of leavin' my bed. I'd never had nuthin', *anythin'* even close to this bed. There was a board for your head and a board for your foot. Me an' Clay had a talk about why somebody didn't name it a feet board, unless it was for someone with just one foot. Clay said he'd never realized I was stubborn, and I said it didn't matter a whit what they called it, cause I didn't figure I'd ever grow enough to touch both my head and a foot! My boards had flowers, pink roses, lilacs and ivy painted on 'em. Martha told me about brushes and paintin' pictures, instead of rocks, or barns, or doors. If these brushes were little enough they could paint pictures everywhere. Nothin' anywhere was so pretty as my very own room, and I never wanted to leave it.

There was a slight tappin' on the open door and there was my beautiful Oatie Mam. All of a sudden I had to yawn and stretch for a minute. I stretched so big I thought I might touch those boards after all. Oatie was carryin' a little tray with some pancakes and sausage placed on one of those plates that would break. She put the tray down past my feet, lifted me and propped me up to sittin', with pillows behind me. Then she raised that little tray and I saw legs on it. She placed it on my lap and said, "I thought perhaps you'd like breakfast in bed the day before your birthday."

I looked and I had my own sweet table a sittin' on my lap. I said, "Do you suppose I'm a Princess, Oatie? I sure feel like it."

"We think you are *our* Princess, but I must warn you, as soon as you have eaten your breakfast you'll need to hop up and get your morning business taken care of. See this darling little bell? Well dear, Martha says you're to shake it till someone comes up to you. Since we don't have help to carry bathwater up here, we have a lovely bathing room downstairs behind the kitchen. It has a large fireplace that holds very large water kettles so that there's always hot water. Now eat up darlin', before everything gets cold, and then ring your bell." She smiled as she went out the door.

I was about halfway through, wonderin' could I stuff more in, when I heard Clay's door open and close. He peeked around the door with huge eyes. He said, "I liked to never woke up. I can't ever remember sleepin' this long, oh boy! Did you and Miss Myrtle have a good sleep in your new bed? I thought you'd want to go back to the box house." He chuckled.

I said, "Clay, I love the box house, so don't be mean. I'm not plannin' to get out of this bed or ever leave this room, so you'll have to get used to visitin' me here." We both grinned.

He waited till I finished my breakfast and helped me get that tray table off of me without those dishes sliding off. I was afraid they'd slide off and break and I sure didn't want to be the first one to do somethin' sad in our new home.

We stood at the top of the steps and rang the bell. Oatie and Raff appeared and when they caught sight of us at the top ringin' that bell. Raff said, "Well I never ..."

They stood with their hands on their hips and just laughed at us. Then they came up the stairs, hugged us both, sent Clay down for his breakfast and started on me. Raff took the tray and Oatie gathered up me and my clothes and down we went for my first real bath in a bathin' tub. It sounded like pretty much fun.

I swear there was places in this great big house that I didn't even know about. I was leanin' back in the smallest tub with warm water almost up to my shoulders and I said, "Is Clay eatin' in the kitchen?" When she nodded, I said, "Can he come see the bathtub room and me a sittin' in this tub? He'll be so surprised!"

"*LIL,*" Oatie said, "you don't have any clothes on! You must learn to be modest. A lady never lets a gentleman see her without her body being covered. What's wrong with me? What kind of a mother am I? I must have thought you'd know that! You must NEVER expose yourself or your undergarments. Oh, my dear, wait 'til I tell Martha and Raff. I'll get a lecture and a half!"

I knew my eyes was poppin' outta my head. Now, here was a whole new bunch of rules I'd be needin' to figure out. I thought I was on my way to bein' grow'd, grown up and here I just got a whole new bunch of how-to's. Seems like every day there's somethin' to learn and worry about. Oatie had been washin' and dressin' me ever since I could 'member, so I didn't pay any attention to that body thing, 'cept to always keep me sparklin' clean. I knew I'd like to grow tall so's I could do more things, but now, I've got this new worry. I'm wonderin' if growin' up is as much fun as I thought it would be?

After Oatie got me sparklin', she said, "Lil, you're mighty quiet. Are you all right? You'll be needin' to go up those stairs and get your bedroom fluffed up and in good shape. Can you manage those steps? Fury said you should have someone with you for a while till you're really ready to use them. You must go very slowly till you've mastered them. I bet Clay would go with you or you can wait and I'll take you up."

We decided I'd stay and watch her deal with the water and straighten the bathin' room and then she could help me with the stairs. After missin' her for a week I was goin' to take every minute with her I could. I knew I had me good teachers, with Oatie, Raff and Martha, and I told Oatie that.

She said, "Lil, everyone you meet is a teacher. Some are better than others but everyone has something to teach you. They may not even know they're teachin' you, but you're so smart, you need to pay attention to everyone and everything you can. You'll see things you like and lots that you don't like but it's all valuable information. You have to decide which is good and which is bad. If it wasn't for people watching, none of us would be half the people we are. Learning your ABCs in a schoolroom's wonderful, but there's a, well, there's a school of life that in its own way is more important. I know that sounds confusing …"

I said, "Oatie, I watch people all the time. I watch how their faces look one way and their mouths say something different. I watch and listen to what they say and then I see 'em do somethin' else. I'm a people watcher, Oatie, that's why I have so many seeds in my melon. It's from all my people watchin' and thinkin' about what people say. I've watched your eyes and Raff's eyes since … forever. I know when you're sad, and glad, and oh, Oatie, I'm so happy. I'm so thrilled, now that I know people watchin' is a good thing. I'll be the very best one."

Oatie sat down and sat me on her lap. She said, "Lil, so much has happened in our lives since we found you that it makes me wonder if I've explained everything carefully enough, but it seems I needn't have worried. I do believe you haven't missed much. You are such a joy to your family and friends, and every day just gets better. God-Willin' must have loved us all greatly to have given you to us." She hugged me and kissed me till we was both giggling. She said, "My very own little people watcher! I am a fortunate mother. Now let's get you up those stairs so you can take care of your chores."

That "goin' up the stairs" was sure a bother. It took so long I was afraid I'd fall asleep. Goin' up was sure better than comin' down, tho, it was really slow cause I had to one-step. She left me at the top and said, "Ring that little bell when your room is straight and I'll come walk you down. We better get a move on, cause Billy Joe should be pulling up before long. Do you suppose he'll really be bringing you a piano?"

I nodded and grinned and ran into my room and Miss Myrtle.

—m—

I loved my room so much that I loved 'fluffin' it up.' I loved touchin' each piece and lookin' at each of the books. I sat Miss Myrtle right up in the center of the bed so she could see everthin'. I told her we were in a house sittin' on top of a house. I even told her we were higher than some of the trees. I thought I heard her gasp, but she's a lady and has very good manners, so she stayed right where I put her.

I went out of my room to that big hall where the windows were. I really wanted to see the tops of trees. I climbed up on a chair and looked out and I couldn't believe my eyes. It was like I was on top of the world! I looked and looked and saw hills and trees and it was all beautiful. I thought for sure I was seein' part of California one way and Middleboro the other way. I was wishin' I could ride Dancer into Middleboro. That would be so much fun. I'd never seen a town, but I wasn't scared anymore. I was almost five, and I lived in this house. I knew I was big enough to see a town. The more I thought, the more excited I got.

I was lookin' at where I knew Middleboro lived and there were clouds of sand or dirt poppin' up here and there. I couldn't take my eyes off of 'em. They was gettin' closer and closer, and I started hearin' all sorts of noise downstairs and doors, and I could hear some yellin'. All of a sudden I thought – Billy Joe! Billy Joe's here, Billy Joe's here! I have to go see him. I climbed down and ran to the stairs and 'membered I needed to ring the bell. I ran into my room and grabbed the bell and started ringin' it as I ran back to the stairs. No one came, so I rang it harder and harder till a little thing fell off and went bouncin' all the way down those stairs. Then my bell wouldn't ring. I started callin' for Oatie, then Raff, then Martha, Clay, Uncle Fury, Uncle Bear – ever'one I knew, and no one came. I was jumpin' up and down and runnin' back and forth. I was cryin' and hollerin' and bouncin' around cuz I needed to get down those stairs fast and I couldn't go fast. I just sat down at the top of them and cried and cried. I hated them, those stairs. Where is ever'body? I hated this big ol' house. Ever'body's forgot me. I hate it and I want to go back and live in my box house with Raff and Martha. I can always get out of the box house door.

    I looked down all those horrid steps, and I knew I'd go fallin' down 'em and crack my melon and who knows what all. I was sittin' there and all of a sudden I thought, bein' down close to 'em wasn't near as scary as standin' up, but they were still scary. The top one was hidden under my skirt, so it didn't frighten me like those other ones that weren't hidden. I knew what I'd do. I got up and ran to my room and carefully rearranged Miss Myrtle and pulled my biggest pillow off my bed. I ran back and sat it on the top of the stairs. I carefully sat on it and held it as tightly as my fists could grab it. I skooched forward till I was hangin' over and I was feelin' that throw-up feelin' a comin' pretty fast, but all I could think of was gettin' down those dreadful steps. I eased as close as I could to the rail and took a deep, deep breath, clutched that pillow and skooched off. It was so bumpy I almost lost my grip, but I held on for dear life and I went flyin' down. I was almost to the end, when the front door opened and people were screamin'. It made me lose my grip on one side and I guess it threw me around and I went slidin' across the floor. Everyone was yellin' and tryin' to see how bad I was hurt, and Uncle Fury and Billy Joe was pickin' me up and pattin' me and lookin' for blood and askin' where I hurt. If I hadn't been so mad and so sad and so scared, I surely could have enjoyed it. I made it to the bottom and hadn't broken my melon! My goodness, ever'one was havin' a fit they was so worried. I didn't feel bad at all. My sitter hurt a little, but other than that, it was purty excitin' and – an' fun! I caught a glimpse of Clay. He had to sit down and put his head in his hands. Seemed like my family loved me after all, but then I 'membered them all leavin' me. Desertin' me! I could have fallen down them mean old steps and smashed my arms and legs and ... my melon. But I didn't. Goodness, they were all so upset that I needed to be grow'd, grown up and let 'em know I was fine.

I heard the voice before I could see her. "For heaven's sake, stand the child up and quit scarin' her to pieces. I'd wager she's just fine. I'd even be willing to say she's just had the best ride of her life. Isn't that about right, Lil?"

I looked at Raff and grinned and nodded sheepishly. Ever'one went through a bunch of "Oh my Gods," "Oh thank the Lord," how scared they were and on and on. I looked into Raff's eyes, and they was twinklin' and her mouth was twitchin' till she couldn't stand it any more and her wonderful laugh filled the air. I was so relieved that I started laughin'.

I looked at Clay's tear-stained face and the frowns on Oatie and Fury's faces, and I was about to worry, but Raff said, "All right, listen up, you two. You need to be gettin' those frowns off of your faces. Instead, you should be poppin' buttons because you're so proud. You've been so careful to teach her to mind, but also to think. To use that head, sorry Lil, that melon of hers. Well that's just what she did. I for one think it was a brilliant move. She was told not to walk down those steps by herself. So she didn't. She had the presence of mind to use a pillow. She didn't take one step by herself. Couple that with the fact that obviously her bell broke, she leaned over and picked up the little china piece from the bell, and she found herself all alone in this huge house and, a-a-n-nd, Billy Joe was arriving! That for Lil would constitute enough to try to fly out a window. I applaud her and her parents. Now put this behind you and let's get her piano into the music room."

She was still laughin'. Nobody could resist Raff laughin'. Oatie said it was contagious – that means ever'one will get it. That must be right, 'cause ever'one there broke out laughin'. Oatie and Raff looked at each other and slowly started laffin' ... finally.

The Wet Walkers

We heard halloos and the Jackson family had arrived. They were just a little way behind Billy Joe. The oldest boy rode with him, and the rest of the Jacksons were divided into two wagons carryin' Martha's requests. Everyone was huggin' each other and dancin' jigs with me and sayin' how excited they were to be here for my birthday. Clay got to tell 'em about my trip down the stairs on my flying pillow. Their eyes all got big and I knew I was real important. I mustn't let my melon swell, 'cause Raff says that's really a sin, but I felt pretty big and those big kids were really nice to me. I felt pretty good.

I was wonderin' where Martha was. I asked Raff and she said my flying pillow had been a bit too much for her. I felt terrible, but Raff seemed to know that and she knelt down in front of me and said, "Lil, you must not be heavy-hearted over anything this day has brought. We're all safe and sound – and you and Martha will be fine. I made her go lay down and she's resting. If she feels like getting up for dinner, she will, otherwise we'll see her in the morning. Now you and the Jacksons get the table set and then you can all have some games and some happy time. I think you might like to look at that piano Billy Joe brought."

I tiptoed into the music room and closed the doors behind me. There in the middle of the room sat a great big flat table thing on three giant legs. It was a dark brown and there was angels hangin' on it and other faces and stuff I didn't know the name of. There was a bench sittin' in front of it. I real quiet and real careful climbed up on the bench. I didn't know how or where you'd play it. I knew Martha played it and they said my little Mam played it; so I wanted to, but I'm thinkin' maybe there were more parts or secrets to it. I was so disappointed I put my head down on my hands and cried. I wanted to love it and be thrilled, but it must not want me to play it. Then I thought *FINE*, I'll just play my violin and leave this ol' table alone. I heard a little sound and there were arms around me. Hands that I knew were Billy Joe's lifted a lid-like thing that my head had been layin' on and there were little white and black fingers from one end to the other. Billy Joe didn't even sit down. He moved his hands over those black and white fingers, and there was Uncle Fury's and my song. I turned around, put my arms around his neck and kissed him till I wore us both out.

"Kin I touch it, Billy Joe, will it give me music?"

He said, "Not right away, Lil, but Mother will teach you and in no time you'll have all the music you want. She started teachin' me when I was just a couple of years older than you. Lil, your eyes are sparklin' like I've never seen!"

"Billy Joe, I am so happy I could stay right here till I can make music." I turned around, sat down and put my fingers on a white finger. The sound it made was the prettiest sound I ever heard. I knew I could play music. I wish I hadn't scared my Martha with my flyin' pillow, but if she needed to rest, then I'd just wait.

I beamed at Billy Joe and he said, "Let's close it down for now and wait till dinner. A cold wind has come up, so we need to make sure there's plenty of wood for all the fireplaces. Want to help me with that?"

As much as I hated to leave that piano now that I knew its secret, the chance to help Billy Joe was too wonderful to think of missing.

There were eighteen people around our dinner table. I thought it was so much fun. Our big table could hold twenty-four people. I loved that all our friends and family could have dinner together. Our little box house table barely held four, but then we had all those big slab tables out by the cook fire that held us and the workers and just lots and lots of people.

I told Martha. She got to laughin' at me and almost had a chokin' fit. All she could say was, "This child is meant for a life of luxury. Make sure none of you let her down or you'll hear from me."

Oatie said, "Maybe OUR Princess in our hearts, but she is also a child who had lived with nothing, without any complaints. She is happy and satisfied with nothing or everything. I will not have her spoiled, and you Martha and you Fury are presenting me with a constant uphill battle."

The Wet Walkers

Everyone had wood in their cabins and we had our dining room fireplace just a blazin'. It was a happy time. I loved all the Jacksons. Tomorrow on my birthday Preacher Jackson was goin' to let Clay and me be Oatie and Fury's children. This birthday thing is so big and gettin' bigger, and I knew I'd be worn out before it even gets here. We're all going to "turn in" … that's a sayin' that just means we're goin' to bed really early tonight because of that big day comin'. I was secretly glad, because I was havin' trouble keeping my eyes open.

Uncle Fury said, "You've all had a long trip, and we've had a pretty exciting day, but we have a small special surprise." He opened the music room doors and everbody gasped and oohed and aahed. I slid my eyes over to Billy Joe and he slid his to me. We didn't even giggle, we just listened to Uncle Fury.

He said, "We'd like to say good night with a little musical gift. This piano is Martha's gift to Lil and since Lil has never heard it played, Billy Joe and I will accompany Martha on the piano. Everyone wahooed and clapped. Martha had her arm around me. She kissed me and headed for the piano. Billy Joe and Fury picked up their violins, and they played songs for me. It was so beautiful and my fingers was just itchin'.

Martha came back and sat down. She said, "Wait till you hear this, my darling."

Fury and Billy Joe both sat down on that piano bench and proceeded to play with all their hands and fingers. They played the song I loved so much. The one Uncle Fury played on the violin and had taught me to play the chorus of. They were the best I'd ever heard. Oatie's mouth could have caught flies and when they were through everyone hollered and clapped.

Fury bowed, left Billy Joe to close up, picked me up, kissed Martha, grabbed Clay, and he and Oatie started for the stairs. He called out, "Stay as long as you like. We need to get these little ones to bed so they'll be ready to enjoy the birthday tomorrow."

I could hardly hold my head up as we went up the stairs and I was wonderin', how could tomorrow be as good as today?

I guess, like Clay's always sayin', "We'll see."

I heard the music. The music of angels. My little Mam's music. Was she sendin' me her music so's I'd know I was safe forever? So's I'd know she was watchin' over me? Was I dreamin'? I carefully opened my eyes a slit. It was pitch black. It was the darkest part of night. The part I loved. When I 'membered me and my litte Mam, it was day or night, there was no tellin' which, cause the box house was always night. Sometimes she'd hold me and sing to me and I loved the sounds, and her holdin' me ... and the dark. I know she's there in the dark somewhere, lovin' me, watchin' over me, guardin' me ... waitin' for me. She was playin' the piano. How I loved it. I knew she'd help my fingers find the sounds. My piano. The music was so beautiful ... the music was the beautiful waltz Uncle Fury and I played! How could that be? I sat up in bed and leaned my head towards the door. Was I imaginin' these familiar sounds? She was sendin' me her love through the music, but I knew in my heart she wasn't playin' my piano. It was my PaPa, oh I loved that. He's my PaPa and my Oatie Mam is my Mother.

I saw somethin' white slide past my door and I hopped out of bed and ran silently to my door in time to see my Mother glide effortlessly down the stairway. The music never stopped. It was soft and quiet, and I heard my Mother's voice like an angel singing along with PaPa's.

I was chilly so I ran back, grabbed a corner of my quilt, dragged it off my bed and headed down the stairs. I didn't want to be shuffled back to bed so I had to be careful and very quiet. I took hold of the banister and slowly made my way down to the first house. I put my quilt down outside the open doors where they couldn't see me, but I could hear them forever. I curled up till I was cozy and listened to my heart's content.

Was she there? Was she wishin' she could play and sing with them? Did she want to tell them she loved them because they loved me? I silently whispered ... I love you little Mam.

I opened my eyes as PaPa picked me up and held me tight. My Mother was oohin' and shushin', and they was whisperin', askin' me how long I'd been there. All I could say was, it was the dark of night and I saw Mother slip down, and I was lovin' hearin' PaPa play, and I wanted to be near them. I told them it was first light, which means it's my first birthday and my little Mam had sent me their names. My Mother had her arms around PaPa's and me and my quilt and she was cryin', of course, but so was my PaPa. I asked 'em if they was sad. They both said, no indeed they was, *were* glad, that they were happy tears cause I was their dear, dear child and

    it was my first birthday,

        and I had a piano,

            and my little Mam had sent me names for 'em.

CHAPTER 13

I must have been asleep by the time we got to my bed. I don't 'member them tuckin' me in. Somethin' was knockin' on my open door and it was Clay. My room was filled with sunshine and there I was, just a sleepyhead.

He said, "Happy Birthday, Lil. I wanted to be the very first to say that. Would you like to get up? The Jacksons'll be down in the kitchen soon for their breakfast. We get to take a picnic and go for a hike. The last time they were here the two older boys hiked and they found a cave. We can all hike up there for lunch and get out of everyone's way. Does that sound like fun?"

I didn't know what on earth a cave was, but I figgered he didn't need to know that.

He said, "It's sunny right now, but Uncle Bear says he thinks there's a cold spell comin', maybe even a storm. I hope so, I love it when it's cozy with all our friends and the fireplaces blazin'. Father says we're going to light every candle in the house for your birthday party. Won't that be something? Are you getting excited yet?"

I told him I was and I think I was, but I knew I was really, really happy. I said, "Clay, I'm going to call Uncle Fury, PaPa." He just looked at me. "I'm going to call him PaPa and Oatie Mother. I had a dream last night and my little Mam sent me these names." He just kept on lookin' at me. I said, "Clay you're standin' like a stick, what's wrong with you?"

He scratched his head and looked perplexed. He said, "Father has always said, 'Where women are concerned, always tread lightly, son,' and I've tried to respect that cause he would know, but Lil, you're just a little girl and you come out with stuff that just stops me in my tracks. I never know what you're thinking from one day to the next. Sometimes that melon of yours is just plain scary."

I said, "Clay I need you to go find Mother so's I can ask her, do I take a bath now or later? If you'd do that favor for me, I'll try to make sense out of all those words you just said. I never knew we was in anyone's way! I thought we were good helpers. Humph."

Clay said, "Now, Lil, don't get your head in a pickle. It's your birthday! There's secrets and surprises and all sorts of things to do before we can celebrate. If you're standin' around gawkin' at 'em, it wouldn't be a very good surprise would it?"

"What else could there be after my piano? I can't think of a thing I'd like to have more'n my piano. It's the best present in the world."

Clay was skitterin' down the steps. While I waited I was thinkin'. What should I do if I got another present? I 'membered when PaPa and Clay came back from their trip and they brought us all those treasures. My Miss Myrtle and Butter and our wonderful dinner bell. How do you find presents to give people? I can understand doin' somethin' special for someone or doin' somethin' nice, but I don't know how to do presents. I'll ask PaPa, he'll help me know cause he is always givin' presents, so he'll surely know where I can find 'em.

Mother came into my room, pulled back my covers, slipped off her shoes and climbed right in bed with me. I was gigglin' hard and so was she. She said, "Hold your eyes Lil, they're about to pop out." I quick put my hands over my eyes, but we just laughed and laughed. I wanted to grow up and look like my Mother and I wanted someone just like my PaPa to love me the way he loves her. I don't need a celebration. I have the best family in the land. I am a happy girl and I am five years old today. That's getting grow'd, grown up.

My Mother wrapped her arms around me and we snuggled like we used to. I loved her and I was so glad my little Mam picked her to take care of me. We chatted about everything that had been goin' on and how we felt about things. She said Billy Joe had told her someone stopped over in Middleboro and said he had passed several groups of stragglers and families that might be Wet Walkers. That almost made my heart stop.

Mother said, "I know what you're feelin', Lil, I feel the same way. We're just getting a breather after doing so much. We're all so happy with our family and our extended family and friends. Well, life seems so good right now I hate for it to change. I'm selfish, I guess. I'd like to have some time, maybe even a month just tending to us and our family. Raff says I'm not looking at the needs of others and she's right. If it hadn't been for Wet Walkers we wouldn't have you."

I was watchin' her pretty eyes. She looked me straight in the eyes and said, "Lil, you need to know what I am concerned with. Do you know what spoiled means?"

I said, "When our vegetables sit too long or if I forget to take somethin' to the cool house or if we don't get things picked soon enough, you always act sad cuz they're spoiled. Is that right?"

She grinned at me and said, "Lil, you've probably hit the nail on the head, except my problem is my darling daughter, I'm afraid everyone just loves to 'spoil' you. Dear child, between Martha and your PaPa, well, it's a battleground. I'm so afraid they will cover you with gifts until you can't see the forest for the trees. Lil, you have not been exposed to bad people. I pray that you never are, but because of that you are an unbelievably sweet child. Everyone loves and adores you, but I want you to grow up able to think clearly. I ... just worry. Because I love you so."

I said, "Mother, my sweet Mother, I would think you would worry for fear I'd have a fit or turn into sour milk." I wanted her smile to come back.

Well we laughed till we cried. No one had more fun than we did. She finally climbed out of bed, got me dressed, helped me fluff my room and hand-in-hand we went down the stairs.

We walked into the kitchen that had seemed so big to me and it was almost full. There was Jacksons at the kitchen table, some washin' dishes, puttin' 'em away ... they were ever'where.

I yanked on Mother's hand and when she looked down, I said, "I think we need to call this the Jackson kitchen."

She giggled and one of the Jacksons said real loud. "She's here." They all stopped what they was doin' and started singin' me a whole song about my birthday. It was called Happy Birthday. I was so thrilled, I had shivers. I was gulpin' hard because I didn't want all these grown-up kids thinkin' I was a baby or a little kid. I was five and one of them, and I had big lumps I couldn't swallow, but I kept a smile on my face. They were all so dear and seemed like they liked me and accepted me no matter that I was so little. I wisht I wasn't the littlest, but I just was. They laughed and clapped and it was wonderful. I didn't know what to say.

I smashed my face into Mother's skirts and looked up at her. She was smilin'. She raised her eyebrows and nodded and let my hand go. I took a deep breath, stepped forward, held out my skirts and did my curtsy. Everyone like to went crazy, they clapped, laughed and started singin' "for she's a jolly good fellow." I was so happy and excited I could hardly get my breath. They were all clappin' as they were singin' and Elmer, the oldest boy, put me on his shoulders and we all marched around the room. It was wonderful. I'd never had such a fun happy time. I guess I just found out it's just the best being the littlest – if you're surrounded by people who love you and care about you and make you feel wonderful.

Fern reached up and took me off Elmer's shoulders. She was the oldest Jackson girl and my very favorite. She always made me feel special, even more so than the rest. She always shared everything she had with me, and I felt so important when I was with her. She was so pretty. She had red hair, of course, and blue, blue eyes and just a few little freckles on her nose. She had really long hair but it hung in soft curls and she always tied it with a pretty ribbon. I heard the wimmin talkin' to Margaret Faye sayin' she had the sweetest nature they'd ever seen. How she'd be the best wife and mother of all the kids. Seems like every boy wanted her to be his, but even tho she was eighteen, she wasn't in no hurry at all. Margaret Faye said she hadn't lost her heart yet.

Raff said, "I think she has a crush on …"

"Ssh, ssh, ssh," the other wimmin said. "It's bad luck to mention that."

It seemed like there was so many rules to livin' and you had to be so careful not to get bad luck, it was like walkin' through a sticker patch barefoot. Nosy as I was I sure didn't want to know about her "crush" cause I didn't approve of "bad luck" and I surely didn't want my pretty Fern to be getting any of it.

Uncle Bear came into the kitchen and told everybody to "Listen up." Preacher Jackson was settin' up all the parts for the "adoption ceremony" on our beautiful dinin' room table. He would surely be thankful if we all were to finish this celebration, so's he could move to the next one. He leaned down and kissed my curls and said, "Happy birthday, sweet child." I loved this big gruffy man with his sweet nature, his heart of gold and the sadness in his heart cause Martha was sick.

Fern said, "Don't move, Lil, I'll get you some flapjacks and bacon and a little bowl of grits. You're the center of all this, so we need to speed it up."

I nodded agreement. She was gone and back with my food in the "blink of an eye." That's a sayin'. It just means fast, but I like it and I use it a lot.

Clay plopped down on the breakfast bench beside me and said, "Did you like your birthday song, Lil? Wasn't that just the best?" I had my mouth full, so I nodded as hard as I could.

Fern said, "Eat a little slower, Lil, I don't want you to choke. How would I ever explain that to everybody?"

Me and Clay laughed, and I carefully ate my food slower.

Soon as I was through, she wiped my face and hands with a damp cloth, dried me off, took my dishes to one of her sisters to wash and said, "Now's the time. Come on, everybody."

We walked into the dining room and there were all the people God-Willin' had sent to love me. I felt tears comin'. Clay grabbed my hand and I saw he was teary too. We walked over to the table where our big folks was all standin' with their faces covered with smiles.

Preacher Jackson said, "This is not goin' to hurt a bit, children, so you can stop lookin' scared to death. This is indeed a fine celebration. You are about to become a real family." He had a great big Bible on the table. Mother and PaPa put their hands on it and said what he said, all about lovin' us, watchin' over us, teachin' us, and bringin' us up in the way of the Lord. They both said they would. Then Martha, Uncle Bear and Raff put their hands on it and said they'd always be there to help Mother and PaPa and to love us, watch over us, and be our Godparents.

When Preacher Jackson was finished, he harrumphed a few times and said, "I have a rather unusual request, but I have cleared it with your parents and they've approved it. I have a request from Fern, Billy Joe and Runner. Seems as though they'd like to officially and legally be a … a … junior … a secondary Godparent, too." Ever'body yelled and clapped.

Clay and I looked at each other with great big smiles on our faces. Clay said, "Lil, your eyes are dancin'."

Everyone crowded around and hugged us, then hugged each other, then hugged our folks, then hugged Preacher Jackson, and I flat out almost got tired of huggin'. It was a happy occasion.

Margaret Faye stepped forward and said, "Quiet please." She smiled around the table at everyone and said, "Tradition has it that when you choose to be a parent or Godparent, you may, if you like, give them a very small gift as a token of your love. There seem to be several little gifts on the table for the two of you, so if you'd like to sit down and open them …" I looked at my Mother who was crying, of course, and my PaPa who was beaming and pulling out two chairs for us. All the Jacksons gathered around, and you could tell this was their favorite part. My melon was twirlin' and I sure hoped it didn't fall off. This was so much fun I could hardly stand it.

They handed me a box from Mother. I opened it and there lay a little gold cross on a delicate chain. I looked up at her and tears was streamin'.

She said, "That was my Mother's, Lil, your Grandmother's. She wore it every day of her life." She put it around my neck and fastened it. I put my hand over it and touched it with my fingers. I looked at Mother and through her tears, she said, "I know Lil, you wish you had that mirror. Well, I brought it down so's you'd have it." I gasped and she held it so I could see and there was my little Mam, her eyes was dancin', her dimple was there, she was smilin' almost to laughin', and there lay that little cross around my neck. It was almost like she was happy that I had me a grandmother.

PaPa gave me his Mother's writin' pen with nibs and a little bottle of ink. Martha gave me a real set of books bound in leather. Uncle Bear gave me my very own halter for Dancer. Raff gave me her little Bible that had been hers when she was just a wee girl. Billy Joe gave me a leather album for photographs. He said I'd understand later. I didn't have any idea what all that meant but he looked proud, so I figgered it was good. Fern gave me the prettiest little box that one of her brothers had made. She covered it in satin and glued little buttons from baby dresses on it. It was so sweet. When I took the lid off, there were five taffeta ribbons for my hair. One for every year I was born. They were all different colors. I just loved her and her sweet heart.

Then came Runner's gift. He said that Clay and I should move our chairs out and face him. We did and he went runnin' and bouncin' into the other room. He came back with a little blanket, which he laid in my lap. "Hold on to it now," he said and ran away again, and he came back with another rolled up blanket for Clay. "Now be careful and unwrap your blanket." Clay was watchin' me, so I went first and I could feel somethin' movin' and I knew. It was my Lacy puppy and I got to hold her on my birthday. They all helped me get a good grip and she nuzzled into my neck, gave a little sigh, and closed her eyes. The girls had me hold the blanket around her so she was cozy and safe. I thought I'd fall in a heap I was so thrilled, 'cept I couldn't take a chance on droppin' her. She smelled so sweet and when I told the Jacksons that, they all nodded and almost said together "Puppy Sweet." We all laughed and Clay held Barney like I was doin'. I heard a whimper sound. I looked down, and there was that darlin' Pokey about to bust her buttons. Her little tail seemed to be waggin' her, and her velvety brown eyes was fixed on mine. That dear little dog was so proud of her pups and was wantin' us to be happy and love 'em. I swear if I was any happier I'd have to go take a nap.

Runner seemed to be clearin' his throat and tryin' to get our attention. Me and Clay looked at him and he said, "Pokey's tryin' to tell you something. Clay, Barney told her Mother that she wanted a pretty name 'stead of some old boy's name. She's been scairt to tell you for fear you wouldn't want her any more, so she told her mama."

I quick looked up at Mother and she laughed and said, "All right you two, Lil's eyes are about to pop right out. She thinks it's for real instead of funnin'." She knelt in front of me and said, "Darlin', Pokey's little puppy didn't really talk to her and say that." We both looked at PaPa and he raised his eyebrows and grinned. Oatie had to laugh a little. She said to Clay, "Son, we all love that you wanted to remember the barn-raisin' and how the name Barney came about, but she's so-o-o pretty that it just seems like she should have a pretty name. Maybe something that starts with a B. What would you think of that?"

Clay was nuzzlin' and pattin' his little pup and he looked up at us and said, "I, I, I'm just not very good at namin' stuff. I couldn't think of anything else and I can't think of anything now."

The Jacksons was all mumbling to themselves and finally Fern said, "Clay, what would you think of Bella? It's Italian for beautiful. I'm reading a book about Italy right now, and everything that's beautiful is called Bella. Would you like that?"

Clay's eyes was shinin' and he thanked Fern over and over till she got that pink shade on her cheeks. I should have known she'd know just the right thin'. She was so sweet, and she was extra pretty and smart too.

Mother gave Clay her PaPa's watch. So now we both had somethin' that had belonged to our grandparents. PaPa gave him his very own first pocketknife, and Billy Joe gave him two silver rosettes for Chance's bridle. Martha gave him a new Bible with a leather cover and his initials stamped in gold. Uncle Bear gave him a new halter and Raff gave him a small gentleman's mirror to stand on his chest of drawers. That was so he could part his hair straight and check for jam and jelly left on his mouth. Everyone laughed and had such a good time.

I wanted to take my things upstairs, but Lacy was still sleepin' and Pokey was snuggled up to my feet. I asked Mother if I could carry her upstairs and she said, "I've been thinkin'. I think you need a little nap, Lil, since this day is borderin' on bein' too much of a good thing. I think the puppies need to go with Pokey and Runner, tho you can hold them now – every day if you like. I feel we need to postpone the cave walk to a weekend later on when nothin' else is happenin'. William says he feels a storm comin' and I think he's right. If you could take a little nap, perhaps Fern will help you carry your things up and stay with you a bit, then we can start our preparations for the party this evenin'. There's hot soup ready, and I think I saw Raff and Martha cutting out some crullers." The Jacksons started whoopin'. "So you can all grab a cup of soup and bread and butter and maybe a cruller, then perhaps tie up the long jump rope. Lil can get up midafternoon and get in some learnin' on that rope and then we ought to have everything ready to spiff up for dinner and our party."

It was a lot of words, but I got the ones that said Fern could come up to my room with me and crullers and a jump rope! Then my party! Everyone was slappin' everyone else, the boys that is. Why do they do that? The girls was headin' for the kitchen to help like wimmin always do.

I said, "Mother, could I leave my things on the table, have my soup and a cruller and some of that rope jumpin'. Then maybe Fern and I could carry my things up. I'm thinkin' if I konk out now ..."

"Lil, wherever did you hear that word?" Oatie asked.

"Raff said I did it one day. She said I was not to say it, but it sounds like it makes sleepin' fun. Don't be mad. I'll try to only say it when I'm talkin' inside my head. Don't tell Raff, please."

Her hands was on her hips and that meant bizness! Her mouth was twitchin' tho, and she finally laughed and said, "Oh my goodness, Lil, what are we to do with you? You and Fern go have some soup and get some of those sweet crullers before the boys eat them all up. Let your food settle a little before you try your hand at jumpin' that rope."

She looked at Fern who smiled and said, "Don't worry Oatie, I've watched over five little brothers and sisters. She'll be safe."

Oatie laughed and said, "What on earth was I thinkin', Fern, you're a more experienced mother than I am."

I looked from one to another and knew they liked each other a lot.

We surely did make mincemeat out of my birthday. It went so fast I couldn't believe it. After soup, I had a sweet cruller. No – I had two crullers. I hadn't known what they was, but I surely would be wantin' them ever' birthday. They had cinnamon sugar on 'em and was the best things I'd ever tasted. The wimmin all got to laffin' over the way the boys gobbled them up.

Raff said, "Margaret Faye, those boys'd eat you out of house and home. How on earth do you feed them?"

Margaret Faye said, "Well, for one thing I don't spoil 'em like you and Martha do. There's such a thing as an allotment in our home. It's a hard fast rule. Now, you can do some creative trading but everyone starts out exactly the same. Actually, it's kind of fun."

Raff said, "Well, spoil or rule, my hat's off to you and yours. You have a grand family."

Margaret Faye turned pink and mumbled "Thank you." I just loved these wimmin turnin' pink. I think it's the nicest sweetest thing I ever seen.

The Jackson boys took turns on either end of the rope and I laughed till I couldn't laugh anymore. They were so good. Fern sat me beside her and she took one end. Elmer, the oldest boy, took the other end. They started turnin' the rope and those five boys and girls was a chantin', singin', clappin', and doin' all sorts of hops and steps till I could hardly stand it. Another boy hopped out and he took the rope from Fern. The kids jumped out and she jumped in. Uncle Bear, Billy Joe, PaPa, Runner and Preacher Jackson was all watchin'.

Preacher Jackson took a big funny lookin' thing out of a bag, put it under his arm and started puffin' in a pipe. The awful-est sound I ever heard started comin' out of it. It was squeakin' and wailin'. Then all of a sudden it started a beat and everybody started clappin' to it. The wimmin came out of the house and that Jackson family started clappin' and dancin', and it grabbed my heart and soul. I got up from my seat and walked over to where that Preacher was playin'. I thought my insides was gonna blow out of me. I was clappin' and dancin'. I was watchin' those kids and tryin' to do what they was doin'. Then I got to watchin' Fern. She was holdin' her skirts up and dancin' that dance as she jumped the rope. Oh it was the happiest, saddest music I'd ever heard. They was yellin', and to me it was better than anythin' I'd ever heard – 'cept the violin. Uncle Bear and Raff started in, so did my Mother and PaPa. Billy Joe had one of the girls get the others into the rope. Fern danced out and she and Billy Joe was dancin'. Oh, I wanted to learn it so-o-o bad. It was my favorite. I knew I'd never have a birthday as good as this one. Preacher Jackson promised me that he would see that I played a bagpipe before I was six years old.

The dinner of roast beef, succotash, roasted potatoes, slivered candy carrots, mashed turnips, and creamed corn was enough to make all the Jackson children want to come live with us. Raff and Martha were the best cooks in the land, and they all said they'd do any kind of work if they could come up on weekends. All the grownups laughed and laughed. PaPa laughed, but I could tell he was givin' it some serious thought.

For dessert, they brought out a birthday cake and sang Happy Birthday. It had five big candles and I had to make a wish and blow 'em out if I wanted my wish to come true. Clay said he'd help me, but I wanted to try it alone. PaPa came to my chair and held me close and I blew them all out. I got to cut pieces for everyone, but Fern took over 'cause I got tired after I cut six. She said she was used to it. It was a carrot cake and it was fine. Raff and Martha made it and said they had so much fun they might start a bizness. They had my name written in frosting with Happy Birthday.

Oh, my poor head. I was a fearin' I might fall asleep I was so full, but Uncle Fury said, "Lil, we have a few more presents for you."

I was sittin' on Martha's lap and I felt like a limp rag. I perked up a little and Martha said, "Open my little gift first, Lil. It will bring a smile to your face."

PaPa brought a package over and Martha helped me unwrap it. I didn't know what it was. It was a long coat with a tie and it was pink. Martha said, "It's a robe, Lil, it's a quilted robe, so that it's good and warm and you wear it over your nightie when you decide to run around the countryside."

Everyone laughed and laughed. I slapped my leg, laughed and said, "Have you ever?" There was a little silence and then everyone yelled and hollered and laughed.

There underneath the robe were little pink soft shoes. Martha said, "Those are bed slippers, Lil. In winter when the floors are cold, your slippers will keep your feet warm, and they'll keep your feet from hurting when you run barefoot over rocks." I hugged her hard.

That was so much fun I wasn't sleepy anymore. PaPa and Billy Joe were carryin' somethin' over to where I could see it. It had a big bow on it. They turned it around and it was a mirror.

I gasped and slid off of Martha's lap and stood in front of it. I said, "I can see all of us. I can see our dimples and I can see our shoes. Oh thank you, oh thank you. I'm so happy." They explained it was called a pier mirror and could tip up or down. I was thrilled.

Uncle Bear came over to me and said, "Remember when your grumpy Uncle Bear said you couldn't ride your horse without a saddle?" I nodded hard and he said, "Well, little lady, you'll never have to worry about that anymore." From behind his back he pulled a saddle. A saddle just perfect for Dancer and for me. My very own saddle. I couldn't think no more. I was cryin' and I couldn't get stopped.

PaPa looked at me, knelt down in front of me and said, "Lil, stop cryin', stop cryin' right now. There's only one gift left and you have to be a grown up five-year-old to have it." I gulped and hiccupped and he wiped my eyes and said, "That's my girl, now close your eyes."

I felt it slip under my chin and I knew. He said, "Now open them." He put the bow in my hand and I thought my heart would stop. He lifted his violin and said, "Ready."

I nodded and I knew for sure for the first time in my life that my eyes truly were dancin'.

We could hear the storm outside, but I was in heaven. As the notes drifted into the stormy night, it was suddenly filled with sharp, jarrin' noises. Harsh, loud, angry voices could be heard. The distant sound of rollin' wagons and horses, a woman's voice, shrill and shrieky split the wind and seemed to stomp up our porch steps. There came a bangin' on the door. Ever'one seemed frozen in place. Mother and Martha immediately came and stood protectively by me, as PaPa, Uncle Bear, Raff, Clay and the Preacher went to the door.

Martha grabbed Runner as he started to go, and Mother said, "Clay, come here."

Another knock was startin' when PaPa opened the door. There stood a very small man with a worried look on his face. He was holdin' his hat to his chest with both hands and nervously circled it round and round. He was dressed in a suit, and I wondered if he thought we were a church! Loomin' behind him was a huge woman with a fierce gleamin' face. She had mean little eyes and a tiny red mouth all pruned up ready to whistle. She was dressed in fancy clothes and a hat with feathers stickin' out all over it. She was as tall as Fury, and that little man wasn't much taller than Clay. Beside her was a boy. He was older and bigger'n me and Clay, and he had a fat face with a lot of chins just like that big woman. It sure made me wonder if they'd been eatin' all the food and that poor little man only got what was left. Sure couldn't have been much from the looks of him. The big woman's skirts kept on movin', even when she was standin' still. I was so taken by the three that I could hardly take my eyes off of them.

The small man smiled a sweet smile and gently said, "F-F-Forgive us for in-t-t-truding, but c-c-could th-th-this be the w-w-wet walkers c-c-c-compound?" His voice was so soft and the wind was so loud we could hardly hear him, and he seemed to trip over his words, which made it harder.

Raff said, "Please come in and sit by the fire and warm yourselves. I am Mirabel Rafferty, and it is indeed the Wet Walkers compound. This is my brother-in-law and partner, Fury Hancock, and our friends, and you are ...?"

The big woman almost pushed the little man through the door. She said, "We are the Benjamin Marsden Mayweather family, formerly of Raleigh, North Carolina. May I present my son, Barton Marsden Mayweather. We are hoping to enter him in a prestigious school for advanced youth, located in San Francisco. He is only fifteen, but intelligent beyond his years. He is an exceptional student of English literature." She seemed to swell up even larger and gave a sharp nod of her head to all of us, almost like we were dummy-heads. I wanted to tell her about all the seeds in my melon, but truth be told she scared me a little.

She looked around at everyone to make sure we'd heard about that fat boy. She pushed everybody forward and slammed the door behind her. Then, almost like she'd forgot, she looked down her nose at the sweet, gentle man and said, "Oh, and this is my husband, Benjamin Marsden Mayweather." She nudged 'em towards the fireplace.

As they started to move, a tiny white hand grabbed a hold of Mr. Mayweather's jacket. He didn't even move, just kept his eyes down, took one hand off his hat, put it down where that tiny hand was and grabbed a hold of it. Out from behind all those skirts, a small child emerged attached to that little hand. She was dressed in an ugly brown smock dress that was way too big for her and her head was down. She didn't even try to sneak a peek at us. The thumb of her other hand was tucked in her mouth. She looked so cold I feared it might be frozen that way. She nestled close to him and laid her head against him. He looked up at us, but kept hold of that hand. His eyes looked at each of us and he looked so sad my heart lurched.

Before he could open his mouth, that big ol' woman said, "Oh yes, this is Mr. Mayweather's youngest sister's child. The sister died birthing her. We, out of the kindness of our hearts and generosity of spirit in the Mayweather's tradition, have graciously given this orphan child a home. I have bestowed the name of Flora on her, hoping it will give her a sense of being. As she seemed to have no Father, ahem-ahem," she cleared her throat, "we are her only relations, or ahem, Mr. Mayweather is."

I looked up at Mother and Martha and said quietly, "I sure don't like that woman and I can only understand part of what she says."

I saw the corners of Mother's and Martha's mouths twitch, which I knew meant they'd both love to giggle, and Mother whispered, "We feel the same way, Lil."

I looked back, and the little man looked as though his heart would break. He looked down at the tiny little child, took his hand from her long enough to gently pat the pale whitish stringy hair of the child, looked at us and said, "I call her Flossie, she seems to like that."

The tiny girl looked up at the sweet man and then looked directly at us, and you could have heard a pin drop it was so quiet. I gasped and squeezed Mother's hand. She gasped, too, but not nearly as loud as I had. We was all starin' at "Flossie." Her thumb was plopped in her mouth like maybe it would never come out, and two of the brownest eyes I'd ever seen, even browner than the beavers we'd seen in the pond, were lookin' at opposite sides of the room. She was *CROSS-EYED! Bad cross-eyed*!

When the folks was here for the barn raisin', two of the older boys laughed and teased Minnie Watkins. They told her she had one eye that was a lookin' at 'em, while the other one was a watchin' the squirrel in the tree. PaPa heard them and grabbed each boy by the ear and marched them over to their folks. He was really mad! Mother explained to us how sometimes when you're born, for no reason, your eyes didn't get hooked up right, and to tease and laugh at the person was a sin in God-Willin's eyes.

I looked directly into Flossie's nose cause I didn't know where else to look, and I smiled big so my dimple would show. I walked right over to Flossie and held out my hand and said, "Come, sit with me, Flossie, I have a doll named Miss Myrtle and she'll be wantin' to meet you."

The little thing's head pointed in my direction. She turned it in the direction of Mr. Mayweather. He smiled sweetly at her and nodded his head slightly. She took her hand out of his and reached out to mine. The other one kept that thumb firmly in her mouth. Her hand was ice cold, but in that moment my life changed, good, better, best. Squirrel in the tree or not, I knew Flossie was my best treasure, my prayers had been answered … and …

… she was littler than me.

www.ingramcontent.com/pod-product-compliance
Lightning Source LLC
LaVergne TN
LVHW011713060526
838200LV00051B/2893